UNDER JACKSON BRIDGE

A THRILLER

SUSAN SPECHT ORAM

SOS COMMUNICATIONS LLC

Published by SOS Communications LLC in 2024

www.susanspechtoram.com

First Edition

ISBN: 979-8-9891982-1-4 (paperback)

ISBN: 979-8-9891982-2-1 (e-book)

❀ Created with Vellum

MY NAME IS IRENA FISHBONE

People laugh when they meet me. They don't expect much from Irena Fishbone, but I know how to fix boat engines. Although I'm a pro at stopping boats from sinking and emergency rescues, I can't figure out what is wrong with my group of friends.

Something is off. Nothing specific has been said, but there is an undercurrent of tension, especially between my new boyfriend and my ex-husband. Another friend has been acting mysterious. My best friend is out of town, so she can't help me figure it out.

They say proximity breeds contempt. But that is not true in our group. We have been close since high school, and we live in the small town where we grew up. We hang out together, along with my thirteen-year-old daughter when she puts up with us. We are as tight as good friends can get, and I would trust them with my life.

Whatever is going on has to be a temporary wrinkle.

1

———

I hang up from talking to my former husband and lean against the white porcelain kitchen sink in my house. Jack called to talk about our thirteen-year-old daughter. I chew on the inside of my mouth and think of all the ways I can get him to pay me the money he owes. I have been waiting ten years, and that is far too long.

Buzz, my boyfriend for the last four months, comes over and massages my shoulders. "What was that about?"

His question breaks my bubble of thoughts. I've lived with my daughter for ten years, and I'm not used to an adult listening to my conversations. I step away and say, "What do you mean?"

"Just now, when you were talking to Jack."

"We were talking about when Kelly will stay with me or at his place."

"Doesn't he have every other weekend and Wednesday nights?"

"He did. He's starting a new job that conflicts with the schedule. It's part-time."

Buzz shakes his head. "He can't hold down a job, can he?"

I grimace, because even though I might grouse about my ex-husband, I don't want other people to put him down. Jack is a great guy, if you don't live with him. And he has a serious sneaker obsession that puts a hole in his wallet.

Buzz crosses his arms. "You guys sure talk a lot. I had no idea how much until we started living together."

I tilt my head and remind myself of the reasons I decided to take Buzz into my life as a boyfriend. He's kind, he's easy on the eyes, he likes my daughter, and he's interesting. More than any man I know, he can hold up his end of a conversation. Being with him is like eating a warm biscuit with butter and homemade jam in the middle. He's delicious, delectable, and earns a steady income as a bookstore owner.

I say, "But you've been around us for years. It shouldn't come as a surprise."

He holds my gaze. "It's different now. I assumed you'd spend less time talking to him when I was in the picture. I wonder if there's room for me in this relationship, given how tight you two are."

I purse my lips and mull over what he said. A nagging

concern flits past and roosts on my shoulder. I didn't expect anything to change when Buzz moved into my place last week, and I guess that was naïve. I know I'm being defensive, but I can't help saying, "Pretty much all we talk about is Kelly."

His blond eyebrows furrow. "I've been listening to your calls. You laugh and talk about your day. It's like you never divorced him."

I pat his arm. "You have nothing to worry about. You're the one I love. But don't listen to my calls. I don't like that."

He shrugs. "I can't help but listen. I feel left out, like a party's going on without me. And I guess I'm a little bit jealous."

I glance at raindrops splattering against the windows. "Why didn't you mention this before?"

He shrugs. "I thought it was a one-time thing, and all the calls would stop when Kelly's summer schedule was worked out. I was looking forward to time together with no phone calls from Jack."

I slide my arms around him. "I hadn't thought about your side of it."

I thought Buzz wouldn't mind, because we trust each other and have known each other since grade school. When my dad was thrown in prison for killing the mayor's son in a bar fight in Eastern Washington, my mom and I moved to Millersville for a fresh start. I was the new kid in class and picked on, but Bud Wiser, who went by the nickname Buzz, stood up for me and told them to back off.

We've been friends ever since, and he was part of the group I hung out with in high school.

I give him a kiss. "I'll think about what you said. But it's time to leave for Craig's boat trip. I'll get Kelly."

Buzz makes a face. "Just what I need, more time with Jack."

I bite my lip and tell myself to let it go. His dark mood may be a passing storm. And I could bend a little and be more considerate. I say, "I've been looking forward to the group getting together. It's been a while."

As I turn to leave the kitchen, Buzz says, "Does Jack owe you money? I thought I overheard something like that."

I cringe at having been listened to closely. I'm a fruit fly under a microscope. The next step is to pull off my wings and see if I show signs of pain in an experiment called love. I lean in and whisper, because I don't want Kelly hearing anything negative about her father. "He owes me for ten years of child support."

His eyes grow wide. "Wait, he owes you that much, but you didn't tell me? I assumed we didn't have secrets between us."

I swallow, and my throat is dry. My party mood fled a few minutes ago, and I'm as sour as a lemon. "It's between me and Jack. No one needs to know. I don't want Kelly to hear about it. I only want her thinking good things about her dad."

He says, "It must be a huge amount of money. Can't you go after him for it?"

I say, "It's tough to garnish his wages when he works part-time and ends up getting canned at most jobs."

"I bet he could sell his sneaker collection to come up with the money."

I arch an eyebrow. Like Jack would do that. The man loves his sneakers. "I asked him, but he refused to part with even one pair."

"You could get a lawyer."

"I might. I've been putting that off and trying to fix it myself."

Buzz says, "Maybe we can figure it out. Hey, how long is this boat trip? Just a few hours?"

"Three hours max, and after that, we've got to get back for Kelly's dance recital."

He says, "The weather isn't ideal for a boat trip."

I shrug. "Craig insisted on it rain or shine. He said it was about time we got together. He wants to celebrate his promotion."

BUZZ

I go out to the car and climb in, getting in the back so Kelly can have the front passenger seat, the way Irena wants it. She insisted on driving her car. It's only a mile to the marina and we could have walked, but we were running late. This being part of a family is taking more of an adjustment for me than I had imagined. I thought I'd slide in, like opening a book, and settle in for the long haul. But now I'm having second thoughts.

I suppress a groan and wonder if we'll ever be a normal couple with time to ourselves. Or will we be chained by her relationship with Jack and her devotion to her daughter? At times I think I've had enough, but then I remember the long years I gazed at her lovingly, but she didn't notice that side of me. I waited for the chance to be her boyfriend, but now that I'm here, it feels like a scratchy piece of new clothing. I'd bag it and walk away, but she's the one I've dreamed of. When she divorced Jack, I was sure it was my opportunity, but I had to wait ten years to claim what is mine. I can't give her up just because she's fixated on Jack, not when I've invested so much time. Instead, I'll mold her and shape her into my idea of an ideal woman. Before no time, she'll be devoted to me and won't answer calls from Jack, like he does every day when she should be cooking dinner. We'll have the fairytale love I've always wanted, partly to make up for all the arguing I heard in my house when I was growing up.

I scratch the stubble on my chin and frown at how foolish I've been. I'm in love but lonely in a new relationship. How pathetic is that?

Irena glances in the rear-view mirror and locks eyes with me. I jerk as if she's seen into my heart and head. I must keep these thoughts hidden. She must never see the real me. She says, "Is everything alright back there, hon?"

Everything would be fine if she stopped flirting with Jack. I thought I'd have her to myself, but I was wrong. What an idiot I was, waiting all those years. She's still in love with him. Anyone would know that by looking at them together, but I missed it. Book smart I am but dumb as all get out in the laws of love.

I say, "All good back here. Nothing to worry about."

Sitting back, I gaze out the window and wonder what I would do if I had those ten years back. She owes me for the time I waited, for all I gave up when my life was on hold. After longing for love for so long, I'm due for a reckoning, and I want things to go my way. This is my time, and I'm going to take it.

JACK

I rub my shivering arms. Oh, man, am I nervous. None of my friends would understand what I have planned. They wouldn't be brave enough to take the plunge and change their lives. I'm on my own, a desperate man pushed to the brink, resorting to desperate measures.

I'll have to outsmart Irena, which will be tough. I'm curious if she'll figure out what happened later on, but I won't be around to find out. I'll miss her and Kelly, that's for sure.

I know I've got big problems with money, but my sneaker collection is my legacy. It is my daughter's inheritance. And the truth is, I can't help myself. I'm a shoe hoarder of top-of-the-line limited-edition sneakers, and I cherish each pair. I've tried to kick the habit but nothing helped. Attending addiction groups didn't touch the hunger to acquire another pair, probably because I didn't want to change. Nothing touches the high of buying a select pair of shoes to add to my envy of everyone sneaker collection.

I head down the dock to Craig's boat and imagine telling Irena and Kelly, "Sorry, gals, I love you, but the love of collecting shoes got the better of me. And it led to the destruction of all I know and hold dear."

CRAIG

We're supposed to be celebrating my new promotion, but my friends are running late. It grinds me to take these guys out on my boat. In my book friends don't treat friends like this and dawdle down the dock to a party. Besides, I'm in charge, not Irena, and who does she think she is, saying we have to be back to the marina within three hours? What kind of boat trip is that? We might as well be at the Fun Forest riding a little kid's boat around in a circle. What a waste of time, fuel, and energy. I plan to make changes when I come into money. I'll have a new set of friends, and these folks coming onto my boat won't be invited back. No more taking advantage of our buddy Craig after that.

KELLY

I frown and stride down the dock to Craig's boat. Why did my mother agree to go out on this trip on the day of my dance recital? She clearly wasn't thinking about me. After this supposed party is over, and I'm done with my dance recital, I'll sit her down and tell her no more. I'm thirteen, and I'm not a child. I don't want to be included in their high school group of friends. I shouldn't be forced to go out with a bunch of grown-ups, especially not before my recital. Where are her priorities?

And what was she saying about Dad? I heard whispering in the kitchen and crept into the hallway to listen, but I couldn't make out what she said. I hope everything is okay with him. My mom talks about being honest and up front with people, but I get the feeling she's hiding something big from me.

2

———————

uzz and I lug a cooler with drinks down the dock. Despite a breeze blowing past, my armpits prickle with sweat. Kelly strides ahead, as if she can't wait for this to be over. I hope I wasn't wrong in deciding we'd go out on Craig's boat for his celebration before her dance recital. But we'll be back at the dock before she knows it.

Buzz looks across the cooler and says, "Let's set it down for a second. I want to say something before we join the others."

I can't help but cringe. After our disagreement in the kitchen, I don't want to hear about how I shouldn't take Jack's calls or laugh on the phone with him. I never dreamed Buzz would be this way when I decided to date him. I thought we knew each other so well that there were no more secrets to discover.

I put my end of the cooler down and wipe my brow. He comes over and slips his arms around my waist, and my stomach flips when he pulls me close. At times, I wonder what my life would have been like if I'd picked Buzz instead of Jack to be with after high school. That is the path not taken, and I'll never know what the outcome would have been.

He whispers in my ear, making the hairs on my arms stand on end. I let out a sigh and nuzzle into his flannel shirt. He says in a soft voice, "How about we drop Kelly off at the dance recital and head home for a little time alone?"

I step back and open my palms. "I can't do that. I have to see her perform. She needs us there for support, along with Jack."

A flicker of concern flashes across his face. He says, "Jack, Jack, Jack. All I hear about is Jack."

"I won't cut him out of our lives or ignore him. He's Kelly's dad."

Buzz frowns, and I glower back.

Craig calls from the boat, "Come on, you lovebirds, let's get going. We don't have all day. We've got to get back for Kelly's big event."

I give him a smile because he cut the boat trip short so we could get back for the dance recital. Kelly waves from the boat. "Come on, Mom. What's taking you so long?"

I carry the cooler with Buzz, and he sets it on the stern of the thirty-four-foot trawler-style power boat.

Slipping on my life vest, I click the snaps shut and step onboard.

I nod to Craig, smile at Buzz, wave to Jack, and give my daughter a quick hug. A headache throbs, and I massage my temples. I'm in a tug-of-war for time with Buzz, and I can't win. When I have time, I need to sit down and figure out how to juggle my relationships. My best friend Abby, who was married to Buzz, will help. She's known us for years, ever since she first went out with Buzz after we graduated from high school.

Craig starts the engine. Black smoke belches from the exhaust pipe at the stern.

I say, "You might want to get a mechanic to see what's causing the smoke. You might need to use a fuel additive or replace the air filter. Or, it could be a faulty fuel injector."

His jaw tenses, and he stares at the dash panel. "I'll be sure to do that. Would you do me a favor and hand out life jackets to anyone who isn't wearing one?"

"And that would be Jack. Roger that, I'll get on it."

As I turn to go, Craig says, "And get him to take off his flip flops, will you? His automatic reaction is to say no to me. But he does whatever you say. At least have him take them off, so I won't have to scrub scuff marks from the deck."

I say, "They might not leave marks, even though they're black."

He looks me in the eyes and says, "It's not safe, and he

might trip and hurt himself. And remember, this is my boat, and I don't take orders from anyone. You know more about boating than anyone else onboard, but keep your suggestions to yourself. I need to concentrate while we're underway."

I swallow hard. Everyone is being testy today. But it is partly my fault for suggesting what to do about the smoke from the exhaust pipe. I thought I was being a good friend, but I'll button it until we return to the dock. "Got it, skipper."

We are all wearing personal floatation devices except for my ex-husband. Kelly is sitting on the settee inside, listening to music with earbuds on. Buzz is standing at the railing, looking over the Salish Sea. And there's Jack, lounging on a bow cushion, flip flops dangling from his feet. He wipes his eyes with the back of his hand. Maybe the wind is causing him to tear up.

I hand him a life preserver. "Craig asked me to give this to you. Put it on, will you?"

He shakes his head. "I'll skip it. No thanks."

I drop the orange life jacket in his lap. "He wants us all wearing one."

He shrugs. "They're uncomfortable."

I sigh. Jack does what Jack wants. "Captain's orders."

Craig calls from the helm, "Irena, would you steer for a while? I want to talk to Jack about something."

Jack says, "You'd better hurry and help him. Looks like I'm in trouble again."

Before I go, I say, "And take off those flip flops. You should be wearing white-soled shoes. You have a room full of them at home."

He gives me a half smile. "But they're not for wearing. They're for looking at."

I groan and stride to the wheelhouse. Jack's second bedroom filled with limited-edition athletic shoes is the reason we split up. He couldn't stop buying them. In one of our final fights before I moved out with Kelly, I said, "You lost your job, and then you spent all of our savings on sneakers? It doesn't make sense."

He tried to hug me, but I jerked away. He said, "One day it'll make sense to you. The shoes in that room are worth a lot of money. They're our future."

I threw up my hands. "That's it. I'm filing for divorce."

But after I said it, we fell into each other's arms and wept, tears streaming down our cheeks. Our love didn't die, and the friendship remains, but our marriage couldn't survive his shoe hoarding.

Craig clears his throat at the helm and snaps me out of my reverie. He says, "Stay on this course. I'll be right back."

I grip the steering wheel and head for Fir Island.

Craig goes to the bow and jabs a finger at Jack. I can't make out what he's saying. Jack stands and holds up his hands. He moves to the railing beside Buzz, with his back to Craig, who shakes his fist.

Kelly comes over to me and looks out. "What's going on? Why is Craig yelling at Dad? What's he saying?"

"I don't know, but Craig sure is angry. Your dad doesn't look like he cares, which is making the situation worse."

A white yacht glides by at close quarters, going twenty knots or more is my guess, and leaving a three-foot wake. I turn the wheel to take the oncoming wave at a forty-five-degree angle, so we won't bounce around as much, and call, "Wake, hold on."

Kelly grabs a hand hold by the helm. Buzz, Craig and Jack grab the handrails and hold on as the bow flies up in the air and slams down, repeating the process. Salt water sprays up over the bow and splashes the windshield. When the sea settles, Kelly says, "Some party this is. I'm going back to the couch."

Craig hustles inside and scowls. "I'll take the helm. What was that other skipper doing, coming so close? Now I'm all wet. We'll stop at Fir Island for a few minutes, and I'll change my clothes."

I bite my lip and wonder if we have time for that. But I don't mention my concerns because he is aware of our time constraints, and I've irritated him once already. This is supposed to be a happy time, not laden with worry with an undercurrent of tension and anger.

I tap Kelly on the shoulder. "We're stopping at Fir Island."

3

———————

Craig says, "Kelly, will you get the fenders ready? Irena, work the dock lines with Buzz, will you?

I say, "You bet."

We flip fenders over the sides to buffer the boat from the dock. Jack saunters over without a life jacket, wearing flip flops. He says to Kelly, "I'm looking forward to your dance recital. We're all going, right? Except for Craig."

Kelly gives Buzz a side glance, as he readies the lines, as if she'd rather he didn't attend and it was just her mom and dad. She says, "Yeah, that's right."

Craig docks the boat, and Buzz and I hop off to wrap the lines around dock cleats. I flash a smile at Buzz because we work well as a team, and he grins back. Craig says, "Be back in ten. We'll get the party started on the way back to the marina."

I say, "Congratulations on your promotion, by the way."

Buzz and Kelly say, "Yeah, congratulations."

Craig nods. "Thanks." His eyes follow Jack as he climbs off the boat and shuffles down the dock.

Buzz says to me, "I'll see you back on the boat." He follows Jack down the dock.

Kelly says, "Come on, let's look around."

A shiver runs up my spine. I'm surprised Craig wanted to stop in this wretched place. The creaking old two-story wooden building gives me the creeps. Heading down the dock, weather-worn planks groan underfoot.

I glance at my phone for the time and say, "Your dance recital starts in two hours. Let's pick up the pace."

Kelly says, "It's your fault you're so uptight about the time. It was your idea to come on this trip."

"I just wanted us all to get together, like we used to. It's been too long, and this was the only time Craig had."

She says in a soft voice, "I wish grandma was alive. She'd like to see this place."

I whoosh out a breath. My mother passed away last year from breast cancer, and she took the best part of the family with her. I held her hand during chemo treatments, and we thought she was in remission, but the relentless reaper returned. I brush away a tear and squeeze her hand. "Me too, sweetie, me too."

"Your dad is locked up in prison, isn't he? What will I do if I meet him?"

I gulp. "I don't think that will happen, and I don't want it to. When my mom and I moved, she kept our location a secret. He doesn't know where we live."

"The idea of meeting him scares me, even if he is my grandfather."

Two tall front doors are propped open, and a draft follows us inside, making my neck cold. I zip up my polar fleece jacket. Laughter and clinking glasses reach my ears. Heavy footsteps thump. A sign points down the dim hallway to the Fresh Air Bar and Restaurant.

I say, "I'll poke my head in and see what's going on. Stay here, I'll be right back."

She leans against the wall. "It's the same as always. I'm not old enough. I'll never be old enough."

I peek in the open door to the bar, where people sit on barstools. They turn and stare. A woman in a leopard print coat holds my gaze. A man with red shoelaces in orange sneakers says, "Hello."

The last person on a bar stool swivels and nods. His brown eyes bore into mine. My ex-husband grins and says, "Sweetheart, good to see you. Come sit with me, like old times." He pats a vacant barstool next to him.

Thinking of Buzz's concerns about my coziness with my ex and our time constraints, I say, "Not today. I'll see you back at the boat."

He says with a sad look on his face, "See you another time."

I walk to where I last saw my daughter. But she isn't there.

4

My pulse picks up, and I look around. Where could she have gone? We don't have long until we're due back at the boat. I spot her over by the stairs leading to the second floor.

"Hey, I couldn't find you. Don't run off like that."

She points upstairs. "I want to see what's up there."

I shudder, recalling what happened here with my friends when we were young.

Kelly says, "Come on, please? It'll just take a minute."

"Okay, fine, just for a minute though."

We make our way up threadbare carpeted steps and a puff of dust rises with each footstep. I crane my neck, looking at the antiquated wooden building. Sailboats are carved into the ceiling. Mermaids beckon from rocks to join them in the sea, despite the dangers.

Each time I go out on a rescue call, I whisper, "Let me

come back alive from this call. Let me help these stranded boaters and come home to raise my daughter."

We walk down a dimly lit hall. Most of the overhead light bulbs are out. Kelly puts her hand on the door knob of what I know is a large ballroom.

I whisper, even though we're all alone, "Go ahead and open it."

The big heavy door creaks open. We peer inside. Filtered light comes through a large window facing the water. Heavy footsteps tread on the parquet floor, coming closer. Dust flies in the air, making me sneeze three times.

Kelly nudges my elbow and says in a quiet voice, "Isn't that the man who was angry about how much you charged him?"

I give the man a good look and nod. My fee for towing his boat to Millersville was three-thousand dollars. He called to protest when he got the credit card bill. "You're ripping people off when they're in distress."

"No, sir," I said in a calm voice. "You hit a rock, and your boat was sinking. I arrived on the scene in ten minutes and kept your boat afloat so I could tow it."

He said over the phone, "All you did was pound in toilet bowl wax. I could've done that."

"But you didn't," I said. "My expertise saved your boat from sinking to the bottom of the sea. You would've had to pay a fifteen-thousand-dollar fee to a salvage operator to haul your boat out of the water and dispose of it."

"What a rip off," he said. "Next time, I'll do it myself."

Now, the man strides over with a clenched jaw. His left eye twitches.

"Come on, let's go." I grab my daughter's hand and guide her to the stairs. With all that's going on in our group, I don't need the extra hassle of having it out with an angry customer, especially not in front of my daughter.

We climb onboard, and the engine thrums through the soles of my shoes. Craig and Buzz are on board, and I smile at them.

Craig says, "Where's Jack?"

I hold up my hands. "I don't know. Maybe back at the bar? I saw him there a few minutes ago."

He frowns. "There's always one straggler in the group. He should know better."

I say, "I'll run up there and get him."

Craig motions from the captain's chair. "Do it. We've got to get underway. We can't stay on Fir Island forever. Slack tide is about to turn."

I say to my daughter, "Stay here. I'll be right back."

5

———

I run down the dock as fast as I can. If we don't get through the rapids and out to the main channel in fifteen minutes, slack tide will turn. As the current grows stronger, whirlpools develop, making navigation hazardous.

My sneakers slap against wood boards. I rush through the open doors and pound down the hall. Blasting into the bar, my jaw drops when I see Jack's bar stool is vacant.

Panting and out of breath, I say to the bartender, who wears her pink hair in a crew cut, "Have you seen the guy who was sitting there? We need him on board. Our boat is about to take off."

She shrugs. "Happens all the time. Parties get separated and miss slack tide." She waves her hands in the air. "Like it is a global crisis. Missing slack tide. Big deal is all I say. Have another beer and enjoy life. Skip the hassle and the worry. That's why I work here."

I drum my fingertips on the polished wood bar. "I like what you're saying, but we've got to get back to town. My daughter has a dance recital."

The pink-haired bartender says in a sing-song voice, "Oh, a dance recital. That makes everything different. Better rush back to town and forget about finding your friend then. A dance thingy is more important than sticking together until the boat trip ends." She smacks the bar with her palm. "But we're all alone, aren't we? Episodes like this just rip the truth bare."

She leans forward, and I smell cigarettes on her breath. I cross my arms and say, "What's your problem with a dance recital, anyway?"

She clamps her jaw shut and wipes down the bar with a rag. "You want to know what my problem is? It's because I never got to do things like that. I've been working since I was twelve. Started out sweeping floors at a corner grocery store. This is the best I can do given where I came from. Compared to my parents, I'm on the top of the world." She flings out her hands. "Can you blame me for having a chip on my shoulder?"

"Sorry to hear that. You've had it rough. I've got to go join my group." I pat the bar. "Take care. And if you see Jack, tell him to get back to the boat or he'll have to find a different ride home."

She says, "What's he look like?"

"Tall guy with a braid in back and a mohawk on top."

"That guy. What's he thinking? That's not a good look on anyone."

I whip out my business card and slap it on the bar. "Here's my number if you need to call. Jack can get surly after too many beers."

She nods and extends her hand and we shake. "My name is Madge. Madge Barkley. And I've seen the type. If he comes in again, I'll tell him to get down to the dock ASAP. Time is wasting, and the captain shouldn't wait for anyone."

I give her a slight smile. "You got that right."

I hurry out of the bar and pound down the dock, sweat leaking from my arm pits. Just as I'm about to stride to the boat and tell the others to abandon our friend Jack, I see him out of the corner of my eye. He's standing by himself smoking a cigarette, which Craig doesn't allow on his boat.

"Hey," I say, "getting a last smoke in? Come on, we've got to go now."

He shrugs, and his weather-worn skin looks leather-like from years of sun exposure. "I know you're in a hurry to get back, but what's the rush?" He inhales on his cigarette and the tip glows red. He exhales a cloud of smoke, blowing it near my face, and I cough.

I fan my hand in front of my face. "Come on, let's go."

In a slow, steady voice, he says, "You all can wait for me until I finish this. No need to panic."

My muscles tense. I just want to get on the boat and underway before the tide turns. "We've got to get back to town on time," I say, waving my hands for emphasis.

"Well, maybe you should've thought about that before agreeing to come with us. You're making the rest of us on edge. I just wanted a nice, peaceful relaxing time with our friends."

He puts down the butt and grinds it under his heel. "All right, let's go. Sorry I'm giving you a hard time. But it seems like ever since you bought that rescue boat business, you've gone overboard, worrying about everything. I mean, can't you take time off and relax, like the rest of us?"

I shake my head as we stride to the boat.

He tugs on his board shorts, imprinted with images of sneakers.

We board the boat, and Kelly says, "This may be the most boring boat ride I've ever been on. I can't wait to get back to shore."

Craig says, "What was keeping you so long? You knew I wanted to take off by now."

While the rest of us fly into action, pulling off dock lines and stowing them onboard or pulling up fenders, Jack leans against the rail looking out at the sea.

Jack pulls out a cigarette and is about to light up when Craig says in a booming voice, "Put that down. No open flames on my boat. I'll throw you overboard if you light it and smoke."

Jack frowns and tucks the unlit smoke in his pocket. "Touchy today, aren't we?"

I motion to Buzz and meet him on the bow. "Do you think we'll make it back to the marina in time? I'm worried about Kelly making it to her recital."

He nods and gives me a peck on the lips. "It'll be close, if we don't run into any problems, but we'll be fine. She can dance her heart away."

Kelly comes over and crosses her arms. "Will we get to the recital on time?"

Buzz says, "I was telling your mom we should be fine. If all goes well."

Kelly frowns. "What're the chances that'll happen? Every time I get on a boat, with Mom, something happens. She's called out on an emergency, and we have to change our plans. I never should have come today." She scowls. "Mom said it would be fun. I'd get to see a new area of the Salish Sea. But it isn't worth it. The view is just more of the same, Water, water, everywhere. The only good part about today is seeing the creepy old building where we stopped."

Jack shuffles over in his flipflops. "Think it's okay if I smoke up here?"

Buzz frowns. "No, it is not all right. Forget about it until we're back on land. You know Craig doesn't allow smoking on his boat."

Jack shrugs. "Fine, I'll wait."

Kelly says, "Dad, you shouldn't smoke. It's bad for your lungs."

He hums a tune and says, "Whatever you say, my love, whatever you say."

I rub at a kink in my neck. Jack is acting odd. The atmosphere is tense on board. Our party on the water feels like a million days wrapped into one, and it isn't over yet.

6

To make the atmosphere more festive, I hand out drinks. Kelly gets bottled water. We motor into the channel just as slack tide begins to turn. I grit my teeth and wish we hadn't stopped at the dock. The current races past, slowing our speed, and the engines whine in protest. Whirlpools form in the water, but Craig steers away, avoiding them.

I go back to see Craig, who is grim-faced at the helm. "Do you want a beer?"

He shakes his head. "No, thanks. I was planning on being closer to the marina when slack tide ended. If Jack hadn't taken so long, we'd be fine."

"I know. Jack is Jack, but it gets on my nerves."

He glances at me. "You guys doing okay? Getting along for Kelly's sake?"

"Sure, we are. And she's strong. She'll get through this."

He looks ahead and says, "My parents divorced when I was around that age. Drove me crazy to be around them fighting, but I hated it even more when they split up." He shrugs. "It's not easy on kids. Be kind to that girl. I bet there's a lot going on inside that we don't know about."

"I agree, and I'm sorry you went through that."

He blows out a breath. "Everything has to be about Jack, doesn't it?"

"Pretty much. We're all in his orbit." I tap my fingers on the dash and stare at the marsh as we go past Deadman's Slough. But the scenery doesn't hold my attention, because I'm worried about getting to Kelly's dance recital on time. I wanted to relax with friends for a few hours, but not at the cost of Kelly's plans. She loves to dance, and her face glows when she talks about it.

Craig says, "Don't worry, we'll get back to the marina with time to spare."

A yawning whirlpool appears ahead, and I think about pointing it out but don't say a word. Craig is the skipper, and he told me to butt out earlier.

He yanks the wheel over hard to avoid the swirling water, but the channel is narrow. Slack tide is over, and we are facing an increasingly powerful oncoming current.

Craig calls to the others, "Hold on tight. It'll be rough ride from here on out."

Kelly comes in the cabin and grips a hand hold. She's

been through worse stretches of water with me, so she remains calm. But her knuckles are white, so maybe she's not as calm as I thought.

Buzz comes inside to join us and stands beside me, holding on.

But out on the bow, Jack appears not to have heard the call for caution. He leans out over the railing, staring into space. His long fingers hold an unlit cigarette.

The current yanks the steering wheel hard, and turns it despite our captain's strong grip. The bow of the boat lurches, as if pushed by an unseen hand.

Craig says in a loud voice, "Watch yourselves."

We've got five nautical miles left to get to the marina, and won't be easy. I frown and blame Jack for my problems. He is the one getting between Buzz and me and calling every day, even though I asked him not to. He was the one when Kelly was young to pursue his passion by collecting more high-end sneakers, despite us being short of money to buy bread and diapers.

I glance at him, clinging to the railing on the bow. If only he wasn't such fun and the life of the party. But he's not being that way today, for some reason. He can make us laugh like no one else, when he's in the mood. Given his glum mood, he is mulling over something unpleasant. I intend to find out what is bothering him when we're back on land.

The boat skirts the edge of a growing whirlpool. Water swirls, circling as it is sucked into the center. I wouldn't want to be tossed off the boat into one of those vortexes.

Engine vibrations thrum through the soles of my feet. The bow yaws, and the steering wheel is yanked to the side. Craig grumbles as he struggles to correct course and steady the rocking boat.

On the bow, Jack stumbles and falls down to the deck. He pulls himself back up by holding onto the hand rail. Out of pride, I suppose, he resumes his position at the railing looking out to shore.

Choppy waves splash up the sides of the boat and spray Jack in the face. But he doesn't budge. Something is bothering him. I can tell from the frown on his face.

Craig says, "I told him to put on a life vest when he boarded, but he refused. With this rough water, would you tell him to put on a life jacket?"

I nod. Whatever the captain says is the rule on a boat, so I follow orders. My rule is if you don't wear a life vest, or personal flotation device, as we call them, you're not going out to sea with me. Landlubbers stay on land without life vests. The cool people like me wear PFDs, and we live to tell the tales about our boating adventures.

"Be right back," I say, taking a life jacket and holding on to hand holds as I make my way to Jack. My pulse picks up. We should be inside the wheelhouse, not exposed on the bow. I frown and intend to find out what Jack is thinking and why he is acting off-kilter.

7

———

Wind whips my hair and pulls it out of my ponytail. A wave smacks the bow, spraying up a sheet of salt water and drenching me. The boat tilts, and I grab a hand hold.

I hunch over and make my way to Jack. He is standing at the railing, and his fingers are white, holding on tight. The turbulent water, wind, and waves have wiped off his cavalier facade. He looks scared.

Compared to me, he's new to boating. I stepped on a sailboat at age two with my parents, and my mom sent me to sailing day camp after we moved to Millersville. But Jack doesn't take the dangers of boating seriously. Everything is a joke to him.

Last week, Jack and I argued about his not paying child support. I threatened to garnish his wages to get the court-ordered amount each month. But he laughed and said, "You should get a better job. You're out there all day playing on the water and having fun. Get a job that pays more. That's the problem."

I clenched my jaw and put my hands on my hips. "Kelly deserves to have new clothes instead of going to Goodwill. She wants to take summer dance lessons. You promised to pay child support ten years ago, and you need to keep your word."

He cocked his head. "The Beevis Extremes just came out, and I had to get a pair for my collection. It wouldn't be complete without them."

"You always put your shoes before family and friends. It drives me nuts."

He winked at me. "But you still love me, don't you?"

I groaned and smacked my head. There's no sense arguing with someone who is in love with themselves and can't see reason. He lacks the knack for common sense.

He said, "By the way, my reputation is what landed me on the list to get one of the first five pair of Beevis Ex's. You should respect that. I have a following on social media, and I'm about to get sponsors. One day, the income stream will make me rich. It'll help Kelly get anything she wants. It's just down the road a bit is all. It takes time to build a following."

I cocked my head. "Okay, just how many followers do you have on Mytube, anyway? Don't you need a certain number to qualify to get ad revenue?"

He scratched his head and looked down at an open

shoe box containing a pair of new lemon yellow Mostest sneakers. The fresh smell of new shoes floats out of the box, and I wrinkle my nose because to me it smells like treachery, self-centeredness, and poison to a marriage.

He said, "I'm not telling you how many followers I have, because it's not relevant. All you need to know is the number is increasing, and my name is my brand."

I blinked and my body shivered, as if a wave rose up and washed over me. I was alone in raising my daughter. It was up to me to pay for her food, and clothes, and dance lessons, and everything else, like a roof over her head. At that moment, I stopped expecting Jack to drop his shoe addiction and pay child support.

Now, I stride over to Jack at the rail. The boat tosses up and down. Cold sea spray smacks me in the face, making my skin tingle.

I say, "Why are you out here getting wet? Craig wants you to put this life jacket on. Come inside with the rest of us."

"I'm in a bad mood, and I don't want to be around people right now. I'm not going in there." He scowls and says, "Your new boyfriend, Buzz, is in the wheel house. You two seem cozy. You can raise Kelly together."

I glare at him and grip the railing. The boat veers toward shore, pushed by the current. The hull shudders.

I say, "We're friends, and my going out with Buzz shouldn't change a thing. We were supposed to have a good time today, but all you've done is frown since you climbed on board. Is your bad mood about Buzz and me?"

His eyes follow a seagull in flight, flapping its wings and fighting against the wind. We all have unseen obstacles pushing us around, but mine is here in front of me, and his name is Jack.

He says, "I've got a lot more on my mind than that. And don't ask. It'd take a week to explain."

Cold water splashes me, and I shiver. Frigid water trickles down my back. With a shudder, I say, "Just tell me what's bugging you, so we can go in the wheelhouse and get out of the weather. And put on the lifejacket."

His eyes fill with tears and he says, "Forget about the life jacket for a minute. I made a mistake. I bet on Shockley sneakers being the next big deal. I bought their stock on a margin call, betting it would go up. But the stock went down. I mean way, way down. I can't recover my initial investment and I owe one-hundred-thousand-dollars."

I latch onto the railing with both hands. Waves toss the boat back and forth in choppy water. A gust of wind buffets my face. My teeth clench. I had no idea his sneaker addiction led him this far down the path to financial ruin.

"Come on," he says, "aren't you going to say anything?"

"What is there to say? That I feel sorry for you? I don't, because you brought this on yourself."

He groans. "I know. But I'm in deep over my head. If I don't pay what's due, they'll take me to court and sell everything I own to recover the money. They'll get my sneaker collection. I can't let them have it."

I shake my head at how precious his footwear is to him. They're only shoes, but he worships them. He never has been one to listen to my advice, but I offer a few chosen nuggets, in case something sticks.

"You've got to get a fulltime job. Pay off your debt. Call a credit counseling service. Maybe they can work out repayment terms. And liquidate your sneakerhead collection to pay your overdue child support and your debt."

His mouth falls open. "I could never do that. Those shoes are my life. It's taken me years to gather them. They're the best of the best. I bet only fifty or a hundred people in the world have a collection as valuable as mine."

My pulse pounds in my ears. I point at him as we pass under Jackson Bridge. "What are they good for if you owe money and have them sitting in your second bedroom? Sell them. Use the money to help your daughter and pay her expenses. Be debt free."

"No way I'll do that. I'd rather die than sell my sneaker collection."

Just then, a huge rogue wave rears up over the bow. Jack yells into the wind, "I'm nothing without my shoes. They are who I am."

Before I can run away, the wave sweeps us overboard into the cold, cruel sea.

8

———

Thrown into the sea, I gasp. I gulp salt water and thrash with my hands and feet. Frigid needles of freezing cold stab my skin. I swim toward the surface and kick hard, clawing at water and thinking of Kelly. She won't be orphaned today. I've got to get to the boat. I swim toward the light, but the current pulls me under.

I tell myself I can make it. I must survive and get to the surface. I can't die now. I want to raise my daughter. I want to see her walk across the stage for high school graduation. I want to see her dance.

My heart pounds, and I push down a wave of panic as I swim and fight the current. My head pops out of the water, and I take a breath of briny air. A wave smacks into me, water rushes into my mouth and up my nose, and I cough out salt water. The sea gives me work and provides a home for us, but the dark side lurks, ready to take a life.

My eyes sting from salt water, and I blink to see the boat better. Sucking sweet air into my lungs, I wave to the boat, which is drifting mid-channel. But where is Jack? He was swept overboard and wasn't wearing a life jacket.

I swivel my head looking around, but there's no sign of him. A widening whirlpool waits to pull me under. My pulse races, and I swim toward the boat, doing the crawl stroke through choppy water. Maybe Jack is already back on the boat. I hope so.

A wave crests over my head. Sea water rushes up my nose. I snort to clear my nostrils and swim on. My hands reach out, bringing me closer to the safety of the boat. My legs kick. My heart pounds. I want to live. Give me my life, sea, for one more hour, one more day, one more year or two or three.

I swim and send out a silent message. Please, don't let Jack die. Kelly needs him. She's too young. Take him later if you must.

I pant and tread water, catching my breath. I only have ten to fifteen minutes in the cold water to survive without wearing a wet suit. Every few months a body is washed up on the shore of an island. The longer Jack and I are out here, the odds of our surviving plummets. Kelly and I need him. He brings the fun to the party, except for today. His foul mood is because of his blasted shoes.

Waves jostle me. I gasp for air and wipe my eyes. I'm getting closer. The boat is about two boat-lengths away. I look around and wince when I don't see Jack.

The boat turns and heads in my direction. Buzz cups his hands. "I'll throw you the life ring."

Kelly yells, "You can make it."

I watch warily, because if the propeller comes too close, it could cut off my foot. That happened to a man in Mexico. I bite my lip at the many ways to die or get maimed while boating. And then I swim to the boat.

My arms are water-soaked logs. My fingers are numb. Frigid water pricks my skin like a thousand sharp needles. I'm freezing cold, but I push on. I refuse to let the sea take me. I won't die today.

The boat comes closer. My chest constricts. I can't take much more of swimming in frigid water.

Craig says through a megaphone, "Don't worry about the prop spinning. It's in neutral."

Buzz holds up a life ring. "Grab this. I'll pull you in."

I drift with the current and so does the boat, heading in the same direction. Buzz throws the white life ring, and it splashes down a short distance away. I swim, expending my ebbing strength, toward it. I can't let this chance slip through my hands.

Come on, I tell myself, swim. Grab the life ring. Kelly needs you. Give it all you've got. Just a little bit farther. You can do this. Almost there. My inner coach whispers in my ear, sounding like my high school tennis coach.

I reach out a numb claw and clamp down on the life ring. Hanging on, I'm panting and out of breath. Buzz pulls me in, and my teeth chatter. All I want to do is climb out of the water and get warm. I need a mug of hot coffee with a splash of whiskey, a warm blanket and to find Jack, if he's not onboard. My stomach churns at the thought of Jack thrashing in the water.

The life ring bumps against the swim step. Buzz jumps down and helps me climb on the boat with trembling legs. I give him a kiss, hug my daughter, and stumble into the salon. My whole body is shaking. My fingers are white with cold, and I can barely move them.

Buzz throws a blanket over my shoulders. "Get out of your wet clothes. Jack is missing, and we haven't spotted him yet."

My throat closes tight with tears. "I didn't see him, but I was mainly concerned with getting back to the boat. I should've looked harder for him."

Craig keeps his eyes trained on the water, searching for Jack. "You did the right thing. Use my clothes in the stateroom. I issued a May Day call, and the Coast Guard is looking for him."

Kelly follows me, and I strip off sopping wet clothes. A shiver runs through me and I shudder uncontrollably. My teeth are chattering. We've got to get to Jack. Every minute matters in a man overboard situation, but I don't mention it to my daughter. I pull on sweatpants, a t-shirt, and a thick wool sweater with numb fingers.

She says, "I was so worried. I thought you might die. But where's Dad?"

I wipe tears from her face. "I came back for you, and it'll take more than that to put me in the grave. Now let's go find your father."

9

———

My knees tremble, and my arms quiver with cold. I stand in the wheelhouse with the blanket wrapped around me staring at the sea and searching for signs of my ex-husband. Buzz sets down a steaming hot cup of coffee. He opens his arms, and I fall into him, holding on tight. I'm a barnacle clinging to a pier piling, and I'll never let go. Tears stream down my cheeks. I want our beautiful life, the one we're creating together and almost lost today. I am bursting with gratitude for being rescued. I want to shout, "I'm alive!"

But my relief is tainted by Jack being missing. He has to be alive. If not, Kelly will carry a gaping hole in her heart for the rest of her life.

I give Buzz a quick kiss on the lips, go to the bar, splash whisky in the coffee to warm my insides, and hurry to the helm. Pulling down the wool hat and pushing up my sleeves, I say, "Tell me where you searched."

Craig says, "I issued a Mayday call and updated it when Buzz hauled you on the swim step. The Coast Guard is looking for him. They have planes and helicopters and ships."

"But tell me where you looked."

The tension in the bridge is palpable. I gulp coffee and grab the binoculars, scanning gray water. My back muscles spasm. The feeling in my fingers starts to return with stabbing pins and needles.

Buzz says, "We looked where you fell in. We drifted with the current. We backtracked and checked the shoreline. That's when I saw you swimming."

A wave splashes over the bow, and the boat judders. My cup jerks. Warm liquid splashes on my hand, and I wipe it on the sweatpants. My arms tense. Seconds are ticking by, and our friend's life is at stake.

Buzz takes the binoculars and steps out into a stiff breeze, his hair whipping into his eyes.

I scan the shore and the choppy gray water. A soft sob snaps my attention to my daughter. Biting my lip, I make a silent promise to be kind to my ex-husband if I ever see him again. I won't berate him for going in debt. I'll just be grateful he is alive.

Tears spill down Kelly's cheeks. I set the cup down and pat her back in circles, like I did when she was a baby.

Keeping the tremor of terror out of my voice, I say, "Don't worry. We'll find him."

I pull her close, and she sobs. Her slender strong arms wrap around me, holding on. I give Craig a look and hope I didn't just lie to my child.

Buzz steps inside and pushes the hair out of his eyes. "No sign of him. But don't worry, Kelly, we'll find your dad."

She wipes her nose with the back of her hand.

My hands tremble. Jack is in danger. I say, "He was wearing a bright blue Hawaiian shirt. That should be easy to spot in the water."

Buzz shakes his head. "No sign of it yet."

My hands clench. Jack doesn't have much time before he succumbs to the cold. The boat plows into a wave and shudders, pitching up and down. We grab hand holds and hang on. I wish I was on my boat searching because my boat is faster, cuts through rough seas and is easier to maneuver. I'd be at the helm and in control. Sweat pricks my arm pits. I say, "We have to find him and fast."

Craig says, "I'll head for Fir Island. The current might've pulled him in that direction. Keep a lookout. It'll be rough for a minute when I change course."

I grip a hand hold. My fingers tremble. We don't have much time to rescue him. I don't want the father of my child to die. Kelly and Buzz grab hand holds.

Craig turns the boat, and the bow rears up and crashes

down with a thud. Planks underfoot groan. The boat sways from side to side and then settles down when we drift with the current. I stare at the sea until my eyes hurt and blink to clear my vision.

I steal a quick glance at my daughter and my boyfriend. We can make this work, the three of us, I'm sure of it. But doubts scratch at the back of my mind. Was I wrong to have Buzz move in? Should I have waited until Kelly grew up and moved out? Whatever choice I make is wrong. There's no winning for a single mom.

I say, "I'll take the starboard side. Kelly, you take port. We'll divide and conquer, with better chances this way."

Buzz stares through the binoculars, his jaw tense. He and Jack have been friends forever. They are like brothers, ribbing each other and making jokes. Until today, that is.

Kelly taps his shoulder. "Can I have a turn?"

He gives her the binoculars. "Want me to show you how to adjust the focus?"

She shakes her head. "No thanks. I use them all the time on Mom's boat."

We scan the waves and marsh grass. Seconds are ticking toward Jack's last breath. Hypothermia waits in these waters, making no exceptions if you're a kind person or if you made a lot of money. We're all equal at the end, and by my calculations, Jack is at the brink of succumbing to the cold. We've got to find him before he gives in to exhaustion.

Craig says, "Sorry, Kelly, but I think you'll miss your

dance recital. We've got to find our missing crew member."

She stares out, examining the shore. "My dad's way more important than a stupid dance recital. I was just doing it because he says it makes him proud to see me perform."

Craig nods.

I say, "He might've washed up in Deadman's Slough," but then I bite my lip, wishing I hadn't mentioned the word dead in front of my daughter.

She blows out a ragged breath.

Buzz says, "I'll be the spotter from the stern, in case he pops up and calls for help. Maybe he's swimming to shore. Or he could be out there holding onto a floating log."

He strides outside, and I scan the water, gulping coffee and gripping the cup tight. My left eye twitches. This disaster wouldn't be dire if Jack wore a life jacket. We could have spotted him more easily. His chances of survival would be better.

I say to Kelly, "With the Coast Guard looking, your dad is in good hands. We'll scour the water and look in tucked away bays. For all we know, he's on a sandy beach right now, sitting by a bonfire."

Kelly says, "And making s'mores."

I give her a smile. "I hope so."

As we approach Fir Island, Buzz comes inside. "No sign of him yet."

His cheeks are flushed from the wind. I can only guess

what I look like, having been plucked from the sea like a ling cod, but I don't care. Jack needs us to rescue him.

Buzz says, "How about we turn around and search the way we came? Then we'll head to the marina and get help."

Craig nods. "Exactly what I was thinking." He turns to me, "All right with you?"

I nod and examine the water for signs he is alive.

Kelly moans. "We have to keep looking. We can't give up."

I rest a hand on her arm. "I'll organize a search party at the marina, and we'll go out on my boat. We have a better chance of finding him with more people looking."

She says in a soft voice, "Okay."

I scan the water as we turn around. A dark shadow falls over us as we pass under Jackson Bridge. Overhear, tires rumble across the bridge grating. My jaw aches. Jack isn't in the best shape. His idea of working out is lifting a can of soda pop to his mouth. His chances of survival are diminishing by the second. He could be knocked out and drifting underwater. I let out a shaky breath.

Kelly says, "Does Dad even know how to swim?"

I cock my head, considering. "He told me he took swimming lessons." I close my mouth and keep a comment to myself because her father tends not to finish what he starts. For all I know, he might have attended the first class and never gone back.

She says, "It's odd, but he never took me swimming, not even on hot days when I begged him."

I tap a finger to my lips. If Jack can't swim, he has little chance of survival without a life jacket. I swallow hard and hope he took swimming lessons.

10

———

I scan the water, and my hands tremble. We don't have much time left to save him. When a head pops out of the water, I gasp and point. "There he is!"

"That's a seal," Craig says.

I heave a sigh of disappointment. Kelly sniffles, and I say, "We'll get a group together at the marina to help search."

Buzz says, "We'll find him."

My throat tightens with tears. I can't imagine our life without Jack.

Kelly says in a soft voice, "He's the best Dad there is."

I look away and don't mention how Jack has neglected to pay child support and instead added to his sneaker collection. She doesn't need to know that.

We chug past the breakwater and enter the marina. I turn and take a last look, but all I see is gray water. I hope he is clutching a big branch and drifting with the current. Jack, come back for your daughter.

Craig says, "Go out and make sure we don't hit the dock, will you? Thanks."

He noses the boat into the slip, and I grab the bow line and hop on the dock. The wind whips past. A shiver runs through me. What is Jack going through now? Where is he? I wrap the line around a cleat and glance at Buzz, who is working the stern line, and we exchange a concerned look.

I climb back onboard and tell Craig. "We've got to get going. Sorry the party didn't work out."

"It sure didn't," he says, turning his gaze to a boat entering the harbor. "Keep the clothes if you want."

I glance down at the rolled-up pants. "I'll wash them and bring them back."

He shrugs. "No need. Hope you find Jack."

Buzz claps Craig on the back. "Take care, buddy."

The three of us stride to the marina office at a brisk pace. I say to my daughter, "We'll eat granola bars on the boat when we're searching."

She looks straight ahead with a lost look in her eyes. "I lost my appetite. Doesn't seem right to eat at a time like this, with Dad missing."

I glance at Buzz. "We might feel better when we get out there again looking for him. I want to get going on my boat and look. We must have just missed him."

At four in the afternoon, dusk is creeping in. The

marina office with a slant roof and wide windows ahead is lit up. I sigh with relief.

Buzz holds open the door as we go in the office and says, "I'll take my boat too. We'll cover more area that way."

I say, "Good idea."

"Roger that," Kelly says.

BUZZ

I hide a hint of a smile as we shuffle into the marina office. Part of me is so pumped that Jack is gone. Finally, I'll have time without him interfering in my love life or my over-hearing his persistent calls. After Kelly goes to her room, Irena and I will watch movies and relax together. Jack won't knock on her door and ask for her help, her opinion, her time, her couch for the night. I am so sick of how he takes advantage of us as friends. Why can't he grow up and get a job like the rest of us?

KELLY

What a drag this day has been. My throat is tight with tears, and I am on the verge of losing it, but the adults are acting like it is no big deal. Where is my dad? I wish he had worn a life vest, like the rest of us. He always made me wear one. I will never forgive him if he dies today. My hands shake. I am frightened, and I want my father. Where is he? Can we find him?

CRAIG

I shake my head as Kelly walks down the dock with Buzz and her mom. What a shame. A kid shouldn't be left without a parent. It is bad enough that they divorced when she was young, and now this. What the hell was Jack thinking, standing on the bow exposing himself to risks in rough water? I should have hauled him into the cabin, no questions asked. This was supposed to be a celebration, not filled with friction, and not a sad day for Kelly. I wipe a tear from my eye. Her dad is such a jerk, I feel sorry for her. It might be best if they never found him.

JACK

I fall overboard, and the shock of frigid water is a million tiny sharp needles jabbing my skin. My heart pounds against my chest like a kettle drummer on steroids. I'm pushed by the current and pummeled by waves. Kicking and clawing with all my strength, I fight to get to the surface.

11

———————

Mike, the marina manager, is at the counter, and we hurry over to him. I often stop in to talk about boat rescues and how some fool ignored the channel markers and went up on the rocks. Or we gossip about rude boaters coming in hot to the dock and the latest weather report.

I say, "Jack is missing. He fell off Craig's boat."

He whistles. "I heard the Mayday call over the radio. So sorry to hear it."

I grip the edge of the counter. "Can you help round people up to search for him?"

Buzz says, "We're going out on our boats. But we need more people looking."

Mike nods to Kelly, who he has known since she was little. "The Coast Guard is searching, and we'll get a group together to look. Don't worry, we'll find him."

Kelly says in a tight voice, "I hope he's alive."

We are silent and sobered for a beat, but Mike says, "If anyone can find him, it'll be this team and the Coast Guard. You father is in good hands."

Kelly sniffs, and I hand her a tissue.

I drum my fingers on the counter and say, "He was wearing a bright blue shirt."

I don't mention it in front of Kelly, but waves can rip the shirt off your back before rolling you onto a beach, stripped of your clothes. I give Mike the coordinates for where Jack and I went overboard and march to a nautical chart mounted on the wall. I point out the spot and say, "He fell in not far from Jackson Bridge."

He adjusts his glasses. "Currents and whirlpools can be hazardous in that area."

I tilt my head toward Kelly, whose jaw is clamped shut. This is the stuff of nightmares, and the less she hears about impending death, the better.

Mike arches his eyebrows and hastily adds, "But people beat the odds all the time. There's nothing to say your dad won't be found alive hours or days later. Jack is a resilient fellow. If anyone can make it, it'll be him."

Buzz says, "The current was running toward Fir Island, and he could've been carried that way."

"We'll take that into consideration," Mike says, "and divide the search area into quadrants." He picks up his phone and texts. His fingers fly as he says, "I'm texting an emergency announcement asking for volunteers to search for a man overboard. Report to the marina office. We'll assign search areas and coordinate by marine radio. This is not a drill."

Goosebumps prick my flesh. My friend and former husband is the one missing, not a stranger struggling in the water with his legs tangled in eel grass.

My daughter says, "We have to find him."

Her chin quivers, and I wrap an arm around her shoulder. "We will. He's got to be out there, alive and waiting to be found."

The door opens, cool air blows in, and people file into the office, frowning and murmuring amongst themselves. Boaters share a fear of falling overboard and drowning while waiting for rescue. A crackle of energy permeates the air.

I don't tell Kelly, but if a person falls overboard and isn't rescued within an hour, chances are the relatives will get bad news. It will be a recovery mission if we locate the body and haul it respectfully onboard. But Jack might beat the odds and outlast the enemy, hypothermia, if he swam to shore and changed into dry clothes.

I shiver and rub my arms. My daughter leans on me, tears sliding down her cheeks. I'm light-headed from falling in the frigid water and not eating for hours, but this is no time to gaze at a ceiling panel and go loose-limbed and limp. I have got to be strong for my daughter and find her dad.

Buzz is showing boaters on a chart where Jack fell in.

A stray thought occurs to me, and I narrow my eyes. What if Jack doesn't want to be found? We fell in together, and I swam to the surface. Logically, he should have appeared somewhere near me. If he didn't hit his head on a floating log.

I rub my chapped lips. He has debts to pay. What if he wanted to escape and start a new life? I shake my head and swat away the odd idea. He loves Kelly. He wouldn't leave her, and he would never abandon his beloved sneaker collection. He loves to stare at the sneakers on shelves in his spare bedroom.

I grit my teeth. What a waste of time, money, and energy. I wanted to name our daughter Marina, because of my love for boating, but Jack refused. When I was in labor, puffing away, he said, "Who ever heard of naming a kid that?"

I blew out a breath. "How about Marianna? Like your grandmother's name."

He shook his head. "We've got to name her something so kids won't tease her." He studied the hospital ceiling. "Amber. How's that?" He smiled.

I said, "I could settle for Kelly with a y."

We nodded and eyed each other. We were embarking on a journey called parenting. Little did we know how our values and beliefs would appear in stark relief, pitted against each other about whether our two-year-old daughter could watch television. Who would cook dinner, although he often was out of work. We found so many ways to differ.

I study the gathered group in the marina office. I can spot Mildred's gray ponytail with the purple streak a yard away. Jasper wears brown deck shoes, worn without socks, and tugs at his plaid gray and black flannel shirt. His nine-year-old son fell overboard last year, and he and his partner pulled him out of the water in time.

Darcy tugs at a green cardigan worn under a puffer jacket. Like my mother, she went through chemotherapy and radiation. Even a slight chill gets to her now. We don't get to pick our expiration date, but if we could, I'd ask Jack to move his to old age, for Kelly's sake.

Mike claps his hands, and people quiet down.

Buzz crosses his arms over his toned body and leans against the wall. To say the man is in shape is an understatement. It doesn't seem right to feel good on a day like this, but I do for a flash of a second and then I focus on the problem at hand.

Kelly wipes her eyes. My stomach growls, and I rest a hand on it. I'm bone-tired, but I want to go look for Jack.

Mike says, "All right, you have your assignments. Get out there, search in your area, and report in what you find over the marine radio."

I say, "The current may have carried him to Fir Island, or he could be on a beach near Jackson Bridge. Let's find him and bring him back alive."

My daughter says in a wavering voice, "Thank you for helping us. Please find my father."

Boaters wipe their eyes and file out the door. Kelly talks with Mike. Buzz whispers to me, "I should've insisted Jack wear a life vest. He'd be with us, if I'd done that. I feel like it's my fault."

"Don't blame yourself," I whisper back. "He did this to himself."

He presses his lips together. "He wasn't the best at taking care of himself."

"Or his finances," I say. "Remember that time we all went out for beers to celebrate our divorce, and he said to order anything on the menu because he was paying? I ended up footing the bill. He didn't have a credit card or cash on him."

Buzz rolls his eyes. "Classic Jack."

My pulse quickens. I wish we could head home, eat dinner, make a bowl of popcorn, and watch a movie. But this isn't an ordinary moment in time. This is a day we'll remember forever. We've got to get on our boats now and search.

I rush over to Mike. "I need an assignment. Kelly and I are going on my boat."

Mike gives me a search area and opens a desk drawer, handing me two granola bars. "In case you two get hungry out there."

Kelly and I thank him. I give Buzz a quick kiss, and we

head down different docks to our boats. With my boat's speed, I'll be able to get to the area fast.

Kelly keeps in step, matching me stride for stride. "Do you think we'll find him?"

"I hope so with all my heart."

What I don't tell her is how he failed swimming classes at the Y in high school. I saved enough to buy a boat of my own with aspirations of turning it into a profitable business, so when Jack and I started going out, I insisted he learn how to swim. He told me he took lessons and passed, but I'm not sure he told me the truth.

My phone chimes with a text from Buzz. "Call me if you need help."

I nod and pocket my phone. I'm unaccustomed to being part of a team, but I could get used to it. Maybe our relationship will work out after all.

12

We hop on my boat, and I work fast, checking the engine oil with a dip stick. Every minute matters. "Looks good," I say, "we don't need to add oil." Kelly fiddles with her hands. "Good," she says in a quiet voice. I start the engine, and we wait while it warms up, chomping down on granola bars.

Kelly grabs two water bottles from the back, and I turn the marine radio to monitor distress calls. If someone locates Jack, we'll hear about it over the marine radio.

Kelly goes out and stows the fenders. We have a routine from going out often and know our roles. My palms are moist. My breathing is shallow, and my chest is tight. Kelly's dad will be a speck in the water, difficult to spot. We might go right by and miss seeing him.

I call, "We're ready to depart. Take the dock lines onboard."

I steer as we pull away from the dock, and Kelly coils the lines, I murmur, "Please be alive. Kelly needs you."

She comes in the cabin, ducking her head, and straps into her seat. "You can floor it when we're beyond the breakwater."

A few years ago, I traded up and bought this racehorse of a rescue and recovery craft. It goes full out at fifty miles an hour, so we strap into our seats like race car drivers with shoulder harnesses.

I almost smile. She'll be bossing me around before she's out of high school. Come to think of it, she could become my business partner and take the company over one day. She has a knack for numbers, she's good with people, and she knows about fixing engines. When this is over, I'll mention my idea to her.

Minutes later, we're flying through one-foot gray chop. An image of Jack waving for us to pick him up flashes through my mind. He might have been washed up in a hidden cove. The possibilities are mind-boggling and giving me a headache.

Kelly holds a chart in her hand. She's old school like me, and likes to study a paper nautical chart in addition to the electronic one in the wheelhouse. She taps the paper in a nervous gesture.

I spot a log in the water ahead and slow down. Logs can float underwater, with serious consequences for boats that hit them. I've helped people thrown through glass windows. A pregnant woman was thrown through a boat window into the sea when their power boat hit a rock. There is no forgetting that. But it helped when I heard she later delivered a healthy baby.

I say, "Our search area includes Dead Man's Slough, beyond the bridge and marsh."

She says, "Something's been bothering me."

I cringe and wonder what she is going to say. Does she wish Buzz hadn't moved in with us? Or did she see me arguing with Jack before we fell overboard?

"Dad wants me to go to college, but he won't pay for it. I don't want to go, and I'd rather do something else. Are you okay if I make my own choice?"

A knot in my chest loosens. "Hon, you can do whatever you like. You're smart and strong and you know your way around boats. You could join me, and we could work together. What do you think about that?"

I train my eyes on the water and check gauges on the instrument panel. I have a hunch if I look at her, I'll jinx the chances of her coming to work for me.

She nods. "I'd learn to scuba dive. And I'd get my captain's license."

I nod. "We'd lay out a plan. There'd be no stopping you."

I must have sounded too eager, because she quickly says, "But I'm way too young to make a decision like that. Don't count on me. There are a lot of things I want to do."

I suppress a sigh. If I was her age, I would have died to have an opportunity like this. When I was her age, my mom worked two jobs and wasn't home for dinner, so I made macaroni and cheese from a box for myself. I can't stand the taste of it to this day.

As we approach the bridge, I slow our speed to three knots, and we putter under the metal structure. "Our search area is coming up. I'll drive, while you look through the binoculars. Was he wearing his metal bracelet? It'd reflect light."

She shakes her head. "He took it off last week. Said he wanted to be free of jewelry, with just fresh air on his skin."

I don't say it, but I wonder if he hocked it at Bill Rafferty's pawn shop. I gave him the bracelet for our first wedding anniversary.

She points toward shore. "Over there. What's that?"

I bring the boat closer to shore and put the engine in neutral. Someone is coming out of the marsh. My pulse quickens. It could be Jack.

A tall man steps out of the marsh wearing a ball cap and carrying a bucket and a shovel. I let out a sigh. He has gray hair and looks to be in his seventies.

The bridge behind us casts a shadow. Cars above zip across the metal structure, tires rumbling. A flash of light under the bridge catches my attention, and I peer through binoculars. Something is moving away. But then it is gone, and there's nothing to see under the bridge but bushes and bare dirt.

I hand Kelly the binoculars. "I saw something under the bridge. Take a look."

She studies the bushes by the water's edge and tracks farther up a hill. "Something is moving in the bushes and through the trees, but I can't make out what it is. Too many dark shadows. It could be a deer or a large dog."

I say, "Let's ask the man if he's seen anyone."

We move closer to shore, where a man is prodding seaweed, perhaps looking for treasures washed up. We step out on the boat deck, and I say, "We're searching for a man who fell overboard. Have you seen anyone? He was wearing a blue shirt and shorts."

The man leans on his shovel handle and pulls down the brim of his blue ball cap. "Can't say I have. Nobody's out here except me. Haven't seen a soul today." He scratches his whiskered chin.

Kelly says, "My dad is missing. If you see someone washed up on shore, will you call the marina right away and let them know?"

The man straightens up and rests a hand on his heart. "Of course. You can't leave a stranded sailor on the beach. He'll need help, wherever he ends up. And it's nice for an old guy like me to see two girls on a boat. You don't see that every day. Best of luck to you. I'll keep a look out and tell my neighbors to keep their eyes peeled. Bye now."

We say goodbye and take a last look around. Darkness

will fall in an hour. I let out a sigh, put the boat in gear, and we move away from the beachcomber.

She says, "I was hoping he'd be here." She opens a water bottle and tips her head back, drinking. "Where to next?"

"The slough and the marsh."

While we're snug and safe in the wheelhouse, scanning the land and sea, Jack could be shivering out there somewhere and waiting to be rescued. If it were any other day, Kelly and I would be laughing as we head to our next destination. I frown and grip the steering wheel. She bites her lip, staring through binoculars.

My left eye twitches. I want to burst into tears and break down, but I must be strong and search. I love Jack, but I despise him for bringing this disaster down on us.

13

I steer away from a tangle of brown bull kelp clumped together. A seagull cries overhead. Although I won't allow myself to weep, Kelly shouldn't ignore her feelings.

I say, "Don't act tough on my account. You can let your feelings out. It might make you feel better."

"I can't cry now. I might miss seeing him looking for us in the water or on shore."

A harbor seal's head pokes out of the water. Kelly always points them out, but today she doesn't. I say, "The slough is up ahead."

I swallow a lump in my throat, because the current could have carried her dad's body here. I can't imagine how Kelly will survive without her father. She'll need lots of support. I'll spend more time with her. We'll have family dinners. I'll look at my phone less. But try as I might to make up for Jack's loss, it would be best if he waved from shore and came over to give Kelly a big hug.

I check with the others in the search party over the marine radio. No one has seen him, dead or alive. I blink back tears and continue on. A blue heron flies overhead, squawking. I glance at my daughter. "How're you holding up?"

She shrugs and looks down. "Do you think we'll find him? It's been a while since he went overboard."

"It's a small chance that he's alive, but it is possible."

Tears stream down her cheeks, and she nods.

"You never know," I say. She winces, and I abandon my cheerleading efforts. I need to let her grieve and not pretend there is a sunny side to this heart-breaking situation.

I nose the boat into the slough and tap my fingers on the steering wheel. Dusk is approaching. Each second ticking by reduces the chances we'll find Jack alive. Searching will be more difficult in the dark.

Kelly shifts in her seat. I decrease our speed to two knots, and we glide into the slough past stands of bull-rushes. A fish jumps out of the water, silver skin reflecting late afternoon light. A beaver makes its way along shore and waddles into the marsh. A blue heron stands on shore on one leg.

I clench my jaw. What an idiot Jack was to refuse to wear a life jacket. I still love him, but we see the world in different ways. Everything for him is about his sneaker collection, and all I see are boats, engines to fix, and drama on the water.

My phone trills with a text. I frown and hope it isn't a boater asking for help, because I want to finish searching our area. I check the phone and my lips turn up a little.

Kelly says, "What is it?"

"Buzz texted to check on us."

"How's it going for him?"

"Nothing yet."

Kelly sighs and tromps out to the boat deck. The wind plays with her green hair. Before that, it was red. I don't care what color her hair is as long as she's healthy, studies hard, and is on time for school.

A wooden dinghy rests near shore, with the bow line tied to a driftwood log. No one is around. I say, "Let's find whoever left this. Maybe they saw your dad."

She nods.

My pulse pounds in my ears. Jack is out there. We've got to find him. I drop the anchor and inflate a double kayak while she grabs paddles. Going to shore, our strokes are in rhythm, slicing through murky green water.

I'm tempted to burble out meaningless phrases, such as, "Don't get your hopes up." Or, "We probably won't find anything." But I clamp my mouth shut. My daughter doesn't need negative vibes now. We have no idea what waits in the marsh, but dusk is approaching, and we don't have long to look.

14

____

The loamy smell of a boggy marsh fills my nostrils. Cat tails sway in the breeze. We beach the kayak, and Kelly climbs up on a driftwood stump. She points toward the marsh. "I see a woman. Let's talk to her and see if she saw Dad."

We follow a matted-down trail, and my pant legs flop on my shoes. I rolled up Craig's pants to avoid taking time to change clothes. As soon as we're back on the boat, I'll get out of these borrowed clothes.

We come to a clearing, where a woman is painting at an art easel. A long gray braid hangs down her back.

I clear my throat and say, "Hello."

She yelps and drops her paint brush, but catches it before it hits the ground. She claps a hand to her chest, leaving red finger marks on her white smock. "You startled me. What're you doing out here in the middle of nowhere?"

Kelly says, "My dad fell overboard, and we're looking for him."

I say, "He might've washed up on shore near here. Did you happen to see a tall man in his forties with brown hair?"

She crosses her arms. "No one came by while I was painting."

Kelly and I sigh. A tear trickles down Kelly's cheek.

The artist holds up a gnarled knuckle. "I did see something though, now that I think about it. When I was tying up the dinghy, a naked man jogged by. Might that be the person you're looking for?"

My eyebrows shoot up, and I wonder if it was Jack after the current ripped off his clothes. "It's possible but not likely. Which way did he go?"

She rubs her hands together. Blue veins protrude from the skin. "My memory isn't so great these days. He was either going to the beach or coming from it. I'm not sure. I'd better get back to my painting before the light changes. Mustn't be late for dinner. My husband is making venison stew."

She nods to us and returns to her work, dabbing on yellow for stalks of bullrushes. "Goodbye, then," she says with her back turned.

"Bye," I say.

She moves her paintbrush, "Mustn't be late for dinner. But I've got to finish this part of the painting first."

I say, "Before we go, would you tell us your name? I'm Irena and this is Kelly."

The woman says, "Not many know me, but those who do call me Melba."

Kelly waves to the woman's back. "Bye."

We stride to the kayak, launch it, and climb in, getting our sneakers wet. Paddling to the boat, we disturb a pair of ducks, and they fly off. We climb onboard. Kelly deflates the kayak, and I start the engine. A few minutes later, we raise the anchor and putter through the slough.

I say, "I don't think the man Melba saw was your dad. Maybe he was a streaker doing it on a dare. Your father would've asked for help, so he could get back to us."

Kelly shrugs. "Nothing's in Deadman's Slough except an eccentric old lady."

I steer the boat and stay in the middle of the channel. We have enough problems without getting stuck in silt. I say, "She was pretty cool."

Kelly smiles. "Cool, man. Let's keep it cool."

I laugh and say, "Call me corny, but I'm still your mom. I love you sweet girl."

She pats my shoulder. "Love you too."

I drive the boat into a wide bay, plowing through waves. It amazes me how in the slough, the water can be calm. But out here the wind is blowing and beating on the boat.

A dull headache throbs. A cup of coffee will clear my head. My shoes are wet, and I want to change out of Craig's clothes. The fabric is scratchy. I want to wear my clothes, watch Kelly's dance recital that she missed, and have a normal day. The blame rests on Jack's shoulders for causing this mayhem.

I turn to Kelly and say, "Take the helm, will you? I'll start a pot of coffee."

She beams. "Roger that. What speed should I keep her at?"

I stand and say, "Super slow, so we can see him. Two to three knots, First Mate."

She settles into the captain's chair. "Got it. Don't worry, I'll be fine."

I hurry to where I keep an extra set of clothes and shuck Craig's off. I pull on thermal long johns, jeans, a turtleneck, a wool sweater, socks, a wool hat, and slide my feet into sneakers. I smile, and my shoulders relax, comfortable in my clothes. I flick on the coffee pot on my way to the helm and say, "Any signs of him?"

"Not yet." Kelly points. "I steered around that deadhead."

I eye a log, where the top is visible above the surface of the water. Running into it could put a hole in a hull in seconds flat. I've plugged holes like that with cushions, pillows, and toilet bowl wax to keep water from rushing in until I tow the boat to a shipyard haul out.

I say, "You'll make a fine captain one day, if you decide to pursue that."

She cocks her head. "I'll think about it, but I'm not sure what I want to do. You work long hours and look tired all the time."

I bite my lip and avert my eyes to stare at trees on shore. "Whatever you think is best. It's your life."

15

When I slide into the captain's chair to steer, the coffee maker beeps. Kelly says, "I'll get the coffee. Yell if you see Dad."

"Believe me, I will." The boat plows through waves, and I swivel my head, looking in all directions. My fingers are white and numb from dipping in cold water when we hauled out the kayak. I don't think I've fully recovered from falling off Craig's boat into frigid water. I flick on the heater, and warm air fills the cabin. My fingers and toes tingle as the feeling returns.

My phone dings with a text from Buzz. "How are you holding up? Let me know how you're doing."

I type with my thumbs. "Okay, I guess. What a horrible day. Poor Kelly."

He texts, "Poor all of us. Hang in there. We'll get through this."

Kelly sets a cup of coffee down, and I pocket my phone. Picking up the cup, I inhale the rich aroma of dark roasted coffee. In better times, our group would go out for breakfast and laugh. But something subtle changed between us, and I didn't notice it until now. I'm not sure if the catalyst was Buzz and I becoming more than friends. Or him moving in with me. Or Jack losing his most recent job. Craig has been cranky, which is why I agreed to go on a three-hour boat trip to cheer him up and celebrate his promotion. But with Jack's sour attitude and our falling overboard, that didn't happen.

I spot a clump of trees near a pebbled beach that would offer shelter from the wind for someone washed up on shore. I'm operating with blinders on, but I have to play my hunches. I pull back on the throttle, and we drift with the waves. "Let's check the shoreline to be sure he isn't there."

"Okay."

We take turns with the binoculars, but I don't see anyone standing, sleeping, or slumped over dead. Waves jostle the boat. I honk the horn a few times, in case Jack is waiting to be rescued, hidden among the trees. Waves push past, beach grass sways in the wind, and the boat bobs up and down. But Jack doesn't rise from the dunes or crawl to the water's edge.

With a heavy sigh, I say, "The Coast Guard helicopter will fly over and hover if they see something. Let's move on. We've almost finished covering our area."

Kelly sniffles and blows her nose.

Putting the engine in gear, I say, "Let's go over the information we've gathered."

She says, "A dog or a deer or a person was moving through the bushes by the bridge. But maybe our eyes were tricking us, with the dark shadows and trees. Melba the artist saw a naked jogger. And that's about it."

I set the coffee cup down with a thud. "Let's check in with the others. I'll say a few words. Then you take the mic and add anything I missed."

"I miss Dad. I wish he was here."

I reach over, squeeze her knee, and turn my attention to the marine radio. I key the mic and say, "Millersville Marina, Millersville Marina, this is Nimbus, this is Nimbus. Come in please."

A moment later, Mike says, "This is Millersville Marina."

We switch to another channel to leave Channel 16 open for distress calls.

Mike says, "What've you got to report, Irena?"

"Sadly, nothing. We talked to a woman who saw a naked man jogging, which is weird. Other than that, we've seen no signs of Jack in the water, in the marsh, or on the beaches."

He says, "Such a shame."

I clear my throat. "We have one more spot to check, and then we'll head back."

I glance at Kelly, who wipes her eyes. This is the worst

day of her life, and I wish I could make it better. The best I can do is to search for her father and not give up.

I ask, "What about the others?"

Mike says, "They haven't found him. They're giving it another thirty minutes and then calling it quits."

I say, "Did the Coast Guard search turn up anything yet?"

"A kayaker in distress, but no signs of Jack."

Kelly's lower lip trembles. She stares at the gray choppy water.

Fatigue washes over me. My eyelids grow heavy. I blink hard, shake out my arms, pluck off my wool hat, and turn off the cabin heater. I've got to stay awake and stay on task.

I hand Kelly the microphone, and she says, "We've got to find him."

Mike says, "We're doing our best. May all the luck in the Salish Sea be with us. Over and out."

She says in a choked voice, "Roger that. Over and out."

Hanging up the microphone, I wrap an arm around her shoulders, and she weeps. Jack is a lean, lanky guy, but if he had more fat on his body, it would act as insulation and extend his survival time in cold water. If he climbed out of the water and collapsed on shore, hypothermia may have claimed him. There are so many ways to die in the sea today. He may have drowned, pounded by waves. The swift current may have pulled him under and swept him away. My gut churns as I steer, and I blink to make the awful images disappear.

16

Dusk is making the search more difficult. I steer and monitor the nautical chart to avoid rocks. Fir Island's run-down restaurant appears ahead, lights glowing in downstairs windows. The second floor is dark, which is how we found it in high school one night.

I turn on my two bright spotlights and scan the water and Fir Island. But my memories take over, and I steer as if on auto-pilot. In tenth grade, Jack asked his older cousin to buy us a six-pack of beer. We piled into Craig's beat-up Boston Whaler that his dad gave him and went to Fir Island. It was our usual group with Jack, Buzz, Abby, Craig, who was upset because the girl he was dating ditched him for another guy, and me.

Maybe that's why Craig caused trouble that night by breaking in through a back door. The air smelled like

French fries and onions as we burst inside. He encouraged us to follow him upstairs into a dark ballroom. Our footsteps echoed on the wood floor. I cringed and hoped no one down below would hear us and have us arrested for breaking in.

"I'll hit the light switch," Craig said. "Here it is." He flipped it, but the lights didn't come on. I inhaled dust and sneezed. A full moon shone through the tall windows, casting an eerie glow over our faces.

Craig said, "Come on, sit down. We'll tell ghost stories."

Jack and Buzz said at the same time, "Irena doesn't like scary stories."

I said, "I don't. Let's talk about something else."

Jack handed out beers, and we sat in a circle. Pretty soon, Craig was telling a story about a dark ballroom where the moon shines in and a creepy man with a very sharp knife is hiding in a closet, waiting to jump out and pounce on unsuspecting girls.

Craig was sitting next to me. All of a sudden, he clamped a hand on my knee and grabbed my neck with his other hand, shaking me back and forth. I screamed, and shrieked, and wet my pants. He laughed and said, "I was just kidding."

We filed out of the ballroom and down the stairs soon after that. Jack whispered to me, "Are you okay?"

I said, "No, I peed my pants. I'm so embarrassed."

On the boat ride back to town, no one spoke. It took

me a long time to forgive Craig for that. I think that's when an undercurrent of tension started between Jack and Craig. Things never completely smoothed over between them.

Kelly says, "I see something on that big rock. Go closer."

I slow our speed and turn the wheel. Instead of Jack hunched over, wet, cold, and shivering on a rock, a harbor seal lifts his head as we pass by. I purse my lips and hope Jack took swimming lessons. If he did, maybe he is alive and found shelter. But I know better from my years in boat rescue and recovery work. The odds are slim of his being alive. The longer the search continues, the more likely this will become a recovery rather than a rescue mission.

Kelly starts to cry, and I pat her hand. Darkness envelops us, and I call over the marine radio to tell the others we're coming in. They're headed back too.

We pass the marshland, but as we approach the bridge, a flashing light catches my attention. Is someone signaling from shore? I slow the boat to one knot and check out the source of the light. It could be teenagers looking for a place to hang out.

Just then, a distress call comes over the radio.

The Coast Guard says, "Will rescue and recovery operators in the area report in to assist a sailing vessel in distress in the vicinity of Fir Island?"

I wait, but no one responds. The Coast Guard repeats

the call for a rescue boat to assist a boat called the Lucky Lady near Fir Island. I bite my cheek. I want to head home and put my feet up. But a sense of duty washes over me. If you can help a boater in distress, you are obligated to do so. We are near the boater asking for help, and it wouldn't be right if we went home and ignored them.

Kelly says in a small voice, "We have to take that, don't we?"

Normally, I jump on calls like this and respond within the first few seconds. A fast response means more money for diesel fuel, moorage, scuba tanks and other supplies.

"We do. A boater is in trouble, and I can help."

She sighs. "Tell them you'll take it. We might as well make something positive happen out of this horrible day and help someone before they drown."

I pick up the mic and radio in to say I'm in the vicinity and will assist. I confirm the coordinates of the vessel and call Mike at the marina on my phone.

"I'm going to help a sailboat near Fir Island, but I might've seen something near the bridge. It almost looked like someone signaling from shore for help. Or I might've imagined it. Can you have someone check it out? It's unlikely, but what if it was Jack?"

Mike replies, "Roger that. I'll send someone over. Good luck with the distress call. Over and out."

"Over and out." I hang up and release a ragged breath. I grip the wheel tight. This is a dark day for the Fishbone family and our friends. When I finish with the boat, if I don't have to tow it to the shipyard, I'll swing by the bridge for a second look on the way to the marina. By then the tide might have coughed him up from the bowels of the sea, leaving him crumpled on shore, heart miraculously beating and waiting to be rescued.

I say, "Ready?"

Kelly nods. "Ready."

We head to the sailboat in distress. Blood pounds in my ears, counting the seconds Jack has left. Tick, tick, tick.

17

Fir Island appears ahead, and the restaurant lights blink off, one by one. The staff are going home. We are near the boat in trouble, so I switch on my spotlights. The bright glare illuminates a sailboat dead in the water and being jostled by waves.

I slow our speed to idle and call over the radio, "Lucky Lady, Lucky Lady, Lucky Lady, this is the rescue boat Nimbus. Come in, please."

The radio crackles, and a man says, "This is the Lucky Lady. The engine cut out, and I need help."

"Give me your cell number, and I'll call to settle the details."

He reels off his number, and when I call, he picks up right away.

I say, "This is Irena Fishbone. I'm off your port side

and will process your credit card payment before I proceed." I name my fee that covers the first two hours.

He says, "Fine, just fix it." He rattles off his credit card number, and I run it through an app on my phone. When the charge goes through, I say, "I'll see you in a few minutes. I'll be coming on your port side. Prepare to be boarded."

He says, "What does that mean?"

I glance at Kelly, who rolls her eyes. I say, "Put out your fenders."

"You mean bumpers?"

"Yes, to protect the boats from hitting each other."

I hang up, bring out my tool kit, check my life vest to make sure the snaps are fastened, and shrug into a foul weather jacket. I say to Kelly, "I'll come alongside, tow them away from the rocks, and fix their boat. Do you want to stay here, or come help?"

She tilts her head. "I'll come with you."

"Good. Put the fenders out, will you? Thanks."

She flops down the fenders and stay on deck while I come alongside the other boat. I put the engine in idle and go out to greet the skipper. He is in his forties, and his face is flushed from the wind, or alcohol, or both.

Cupping my hands so he can hear me over the wind, I say, "I'll lash your boat to mine and tow you away from the rocks."

His eyes grow wide and he looks behind him. About fifty yards away is a rock waiting to make a gash in his fifty-foot sailboat. A sinking boat is not what I want to deal with tonight. I lash the boats together at midships.

He puts his head in his hands. "I'm new to boating and never guessed this would happen. I just bought the boat yesterday."

I cock my head. It has been a stressful day, and this situation is taxing my patience. I'd like to go back and start over. We should have never stepped on Craig's boat with a dance recital to attend. I was wrong to insist we go. This is all my fault. But maybe the same thing would have happened if Kelly and I had stayed on shore. Jack still would have fallen overboard, and we'd be searching for him in that alternate universe, caught in the same exhausting nightmare.

The boats bob up and down, shoved by waves. The fenders Kelly dropped down groan from being squeezed between the two boats. I step to the helm and steer us away from the rocks, leaving Fir Island and the dark memories it holds behind. I would have dropped Craig as a friend after his stunt grabbing my neck and shaking me, but he was integral to our group. There was no way to cut him out. And I figured everyone makes mistakes, and maybe I shouldn't be so sensitive. I shook it off and moved on.

In a wide bay, I pull back on the throttle, and we drift in what is now a slow-moving current. Trees on shore and the island protect us from the wind, so this is a good place to assess his engine problem and fix it. He is green, and

I'm on my own, which is what I'm accustomed to. Scanning the black water, I hope Jack managed to survive and beat the odds.

I haul my tool kit out on deck and say to the skipper, "Permission to come aboard?"

He wipes his brow. "Permission granted."

18

Wind whistles past, tugging at my jacket. Water splashes up between the boats. I grab my tool kit and step onto the sailboat, setting my tool kit down with a thud. I nod to Kelly, and she steps across the gap to stand by my side. I say, "This is my assistant."

The skipper is about my age, forty years old, and his hands are shaking. He frowns, as anyone would in his situation. Two women dressed in thin thigh-high dresses shiver and rub their arms in the night wind. Their high heels have left marks on the boat deck. A man sits watching with his arms crossed. The four party-goers look frosted that their fun boat trip was blighted by engine failure. We're all having a rough day from ruined boat trips.

"Tell me what happened," I say to the skipper.

"We were going along, and the engine spluttered and

quit. I tried starting it, over and over, but it smelled like gas and wouldn't go."

The women fan their hands in front of their faces. "It smelled awful."

"Could be a fouled spark plug," I say, opening the engine compartment. "Let's take a look."

The cover over the engine is cool, because they've been stopped for so long. I click on my flashlight and pull out a spark plug.

"Carbon build-up in the spark plug is the culprit," I say to the skipper. "Kelly, give me the wire brush, if you would, please."

She hands it over, and I clean the spark plugs, scrubbing off the carbon. While I work, I say to the skipper, "Did you get the boat surveyed before you bought it?"

He cocks his head. "Survey?"

I say, "An inspection? Did you have it hauled out and the bottom checked? Did a mechanic go over the engine to make sure it's in good shape and has been well-maintained?"

He clears his throat. "Not really. I had a friend go on the sea trial with me. He said it was a great boat."

I say, "If you ever buy another boat, I suggest you hire a marine surveyor to look over it first. You never know what they'll find, like dry rot."

He runs a hand through his hair. "This isn't working out like I thought it would. I got in and drove it like a car, but the steering wheel didn't respond the same way.

Coming into Fir Island, I hit the dock. This is more trouble than it's worth. All I wanted was to take my friends out for a good time. Do you want to buy a boat?"

I laugh and put the last spark plug in place, wiping my hands on a rag. "No thanks. Take a boating class. Get one-on-one instruction. You'll learn, but it takes time. And there's always more to learn, which is why I like it." I pack up my gear and mull over how it is better to be a cautious, informed boater than a novice who rams into rocks and docks.

He folds his arms. "How long have you been doing this?"

I tuck the oily rag in the tool kit and snap it shut. "A long time. I started out when I was young helping my dad fix engines. Now it comes as second nature."

The wind gusts, and the boats rock back and forth. Waves splash up the sides of the sailboat. I wonder if the Coast Guard helicopter is still searching in the dark, or if they gave up until morning.

I say, "Start the engine, and I suggest you head into the marina. The weather forecast says a storm front is moving in."

He starts the engine and says, "Believe me, I will. I've had enough of this for today."

I hand him my card. "Call if you run into problems again."

He studies the card. "Irena Fishbone. Are you related to Jack Fishbone?"

When we divorced, I didn't bother to change my name. It was too much hassle, and I wanted Kelly and I to share the same last name. I say, "I was. He's my ex-husband."

The skipper grins. "He comes into my store all the time to buy sneakers. His purchases almost paid for this boat. You know, he says he never wears them."

Kelly says in tight voice, "That's my dad. He fell overboard, and he's missing. We were looking for him when we heard your distress call."

The man's eyes grow wide. "I'm sorry to hear that. I hope you find him fast. This makes my boating problems seem small in comparison."

Kelly nods and wipes her nose on the back of her hand.

I turn to go and stop to say, "Get a mechanic to look over the engine. You might need to flush the antifreeze and change the oil."

"I'll do that." He starts the engine and it purrs.

I lug my tool kit to my boat, which I left idling in case I had to jump back onboard and steer us away from a hazard. The boats heave in the swell. The fenders moan, squeezed between two boats bobbing up and down.

"So long," I say.

"Thanks," the skipper calls.

I hustle inside, stow my tools, and hang my jacket on the back of the captain's chair. I say to Kelly, "Prepare to depart. Go work your magic."

"I'm on it."

She releases the lines and coils them as we move away from Lucky Lady. We crawl along at two knots. When we're three boat lengths away, I bring our speed up to five knots, and then eight. I aim the spotlight dead ahead at the dark black water, so I can see a floating body or a log before we hit it. Foresight helps but doesn't always work. Freak accidents happen, like being swept overboard.

A two-level party boat chugs by. Lights twinkle. Music blares. People dance on the deck, ignoring the chilly night air. They're having fun, but Kelly and I are missing a loved one who, we hope, is struggling to survive somewhere. When Jack is found, I'm sure he'll regale us with tales of his ordeal.

Jackson Bridge looms ahead, and I slow our speed. Kelly uses the binoculars to scan the hillside and beach.

I say, "See anything?"

She shakes her head. "Lots of nothing, unfortunately."

I aim a spotlight on the stony beach. No sign of Jack. At least his body isn't prone on the stones. My arms are heavy as I steer. Tomorrow, I'll look with fresh energy, but right now, I just want to go home and get a warm hug from Buzz.

"Why don't you check with the others on the radio," I say. "I'll steer."

She picks up the mic and says over the marine radio, "This is Nimbus, this is Nimbus. Come in if you're with the search party looking for Jack Fishbone."

Buzz and Mike come on the line, and they switch to

another channel, leaving Channel 16 open for distress calls.

Kelly says, "Has anyone seen my dad?"

"Not yet," Mike says. "The Coast Guard is still looking."

Buzz says, "I went to the bridge but didn't see anyone. Not on shore, not in the woods, not in the water. I came up short everywhere I looked."

If we weren't in dire straits, I might crack a joke about being short. But I don't, because this is deadly serious. Kelly's lips quiver, and she hands me the mic.

I say, "We're calling it quits and coming in. Let's talk tomorrow about next steps."

Mike says, "Roger that. Go home and get warm."

"See you at home," Buzz says. "Stay safe."

"Over and out," I say, hanging up the microphone. I'm glad he'll be there to welcome us home. With him by my side, I'm less alone in this ugly mess.

The marina appears ahead. My eyes ache from straining to see drifting logs and dead bodies. "We'll do everything we can to find your father."

19

I dock the boat, and we tie up, lashing lines to cleats, working in silence. Our hearts are broken, but my daughter needs support after an anguishing day. We walk to my car, and I rest a hand on her shoulder. "Do you want a friend to come over? Would that make you feel better?"

She shakes her head. "My friends wouldn't understand what I'm going through."

We climb in the car. Our stomachs growl. She pulls out a granola bar and chomps down, chewing slowly. Crumpling the wrapper into a ball, she lets it fall to the floor. Normally I'd tell her to pick it up, but I clamp my mouth shut.

She stares out the window and says, "Does Dad know how to swim?"

I take a quick breath, because I was mulling that over. "He told me he took lessons and passed the swim test. But I'm not sure. What do you think?"

She studies my face. "I've never seen him swim. Isn't that odd, given where we live, with water all around us? Do you think he's afraid of the water?"

I shrug. "Maybe. He told me his dad was caught in a rogue wave off the Oregon Coast and was dragged out to sea. He hailed a boat passing by and was brought back to land in a miraculous rescue."

"I didn't know that. I wonder if he has other secrets I don't know about."

I don't share the secret he told me about his debt. His daughter doesn't need to know that. I say, "Everyone has secrets, don't you think?" I turn the corner and head to our house.

She says, "Buzz is nice, but he's not my father."

"No one could replace your father."

She wrinkles her nose. "I feel like you and Dad love each other but hate each other, from the way you sound when you talk."

I park the car in front of my brown shingled one-story home. "I'll never stop loving him. I just couldn't live with him or share expenses." I turn off the engine and it pings.

She says, "Because of the sneakers?"

"Yeah, the shoes did us in."

We climb out of the car and go up the paved front path.

Kelly says, "I'd have my own bedroom there if he didn't have all those shoes."

"That would be better."

Buzz opens the door, and the smell of something cooking makes my mouth water. He says, "I'm making dinner. Go warm up by the fire."

His dog bounds over and rubs against our legs. Happy is a yellow Labrador retriever who likes to chase balls. Kelly and I stand by the living room fireplace before a blazing fire, rubbing our hands together. Tense muscles in my back begin to relax as the warmth seeps in.

Buzz hands us mugs of peppermint tea. Wrapping my cold fingers around the cup, I say, "Thanks, I could get used to this princess treatment."

"Just until Jack comes back," he says, going in the kitchen. "Then he'll need all your attention."

I arch an eyebrow. Was he taking a potshot at how close Jack and I are? If I didn't know Buzz as well, I'd suspect him of having a raging case of jealousy. I massage my left temple. I might be imagining his snarky undertone, but I'll watch for it from now on.

Kelly goes into her room. I stare at the flickering orange flames in the fireplace and make a plan for tomorrow. I'll check the channels and bays and search his apartment for clues about his debt. He owes me money, and his daughter deserves to have a father in her life. We need him to be alive.

The last of the warm tea slides down my parched

throat. I take off my coat and hang it up. In my bedroom, I slide my feet into sheepskin slippers and pull a robe over my sweater and jeans.

I hurry to the kitchen to help, and Buzz calls, "Dinner is ready." Happy thumps his tail against a kitchen chair. Buzz says, "Go ahead and sit."

Kelly and I slide into seats. A glass of red wine sits at my place, along with water. I sip the wine, and my mouth puckers at the tart taste. Buzz sets down three bowls filled with pasta, meatballs, and topped with a red marinara sauce and parmesan cheese. He says, "Eat before it gets cold."

We dig in. Forks clang against pottery bowls. I groan and chew a bite of pasta, browned meatballs, and tomato sauce. Taking a sip of water, I say, "This is so good. Thank you. What did you see when you were searching?"

Kelly puts down her fork. "Any signs of my dad?"

Buzz runs a hand through his hair. "I didn't see much."

Kelly grips the table edge.

He says, "But I did find a hat in the water, a baseball cap, but he wasn't wearing one today. Was he?"

"I don't remember him wearing one," I say.

Kelly says, "He was at first, but he gave it to me, and it flew off my head and landed in the water."

I glance at Buzz. I like how he cracks jokes and makes me laugh. His brown eyes remind me of a puppy's, with undying affection. I love how he cares for Kelly and me.

When he asked me out, I thought of him as a friend. But the first kiss on the lips changed everything on my front doorstep. The man knows how to kiss.

He holds my gaze, and I get the feeling he wants to tell me something, but not in front of my daughter. He says, "Jack's name was on the inside in black magic marker. We bought the same hat and kept getting them mixed up, so he marked his."

He shifts in his seat, and the chair creaks. I sit back. Kelly wipes her mouth on a napkin and says, "I want to know the truth. Don't hide anything."

Buzz turns to me.

I say, "She's right. Don't hold back. It's her father we're talking about."

Happy pads over and nuzzles Kelly's hand. She rubs his ears.

He looks at Kelly and says, "Might be easier if you didn't hear."

She leans in and rests her elbows on the table. "Tell me."

He whooshes out a breath. "I found Jack's hat. But what's bothering me is there was a dark stain inside, like it was blood-soaked." Buzz shrugs. "I'm no expert, but that's what it looked like to me. I gave it to the Coast Guard when they stopped by the marina. I called the police, but they said he hasn't been missing long enough to file a missing person's report."

I give Buzz a glance. "I'm glad you called them. I'll try again tomorrow."

Kelly chews on a fingernail.

Buzz says, "Anyone up for popcorn and a movie? It'll get our mind off things."

Kelly sighs. "I guess. Mom and I will do the dishes. You cooked. That's the deal in this house. But not at Dad's because he doesn't like rules."

My mind wanders to the overdue child support. Each time I have picked up the phone to call an attorney about it, Jack magically appears on my doorstep, asking to see Kelly on the spur of the moment. He and I were like that, with an almost telepathic communication. I understand how that connection would irritate Buzz.

Buzz says, "I'll help. We'll get it done faster."

Buzz scrubs pots and pans, Kelly dries, and I put them away. I say, "I've got a plan for tomorrow."

Kelly picks at her sweater.

Buzz says, "What're you thinking?"

I say, "I'll go out first thing to look for him."

Kelly says, "I'll go with you."

I shake my head. "You have to go to school."

She crosses her arms. "I won't be able to concentrate. Let me come with you."

"Nope, you need to keep up your routine. Besides, I'll be up and gone before first light." I turn to Buzz, who is strangely silent. "Can you make sure she gets to school in the morning?"

"Sure. I'd go with you, but I need to get to the bookstore."

I bite my lip. "I have to get fuel though. I'm down to my last third of a tank."

Kelly says, "A third for going out, a third for coming back, a third for reserve."

I give her a smile. "That's right."

Buzz says, "For all we know, he's hitchhiking to his apartment now."

I glare at him for raising my daughter's hopes before they'll come crashing down.

Kelly's eyes light up. "I want to check his apartment. He might be there."

I chew the inside of my cheek. He is most likely dead, but I don't tell her that. I say, "I doubt he's at his place. Someone would've seen him walking there and told us."

Kelly frowns. "We have to check the apartment."

I say, "Tell you what, after I search tomorrow morning, I'll stop at his place and take a look."

Kelly pulls out her phone. "I'll call him. I should've done this before."

She dials, and the line rings. Buzz and I exchange a concerned look. If Jack is dead, the news will devastate Kelly. But until we find his body, the waiting will be agony.

Kelly hangs up and rubs her eyes. "Maybe he's in the shower."

Buzz and I are quiet. Denial is a powerful delusion, offering comfort.

Kelly says, "He can't be dead. He's my dad."

I open my arms, and she sobs. I mouth the words over her shoulder to Buzz, "I love you." He sends me an air kiss and leaves the room. I resolve to follow through with my plans for tomorrow. Kelly is sinking, and I must save her.

20

———

I toss and turn in bed. The covers are heavy, making me hot, and I push them off. Buzz snores next to me. I slip out of bed and pad to the bathroom. A cool breeze brings briny air through a cracked open window.

I close the bathroom door, keeping the light off so as not to wake Buzz. He's good with Kelly and takes her to dance class when I have to be on the boat working. I know Buzz as well as my boat engine. I'm sure he doesn't have any secrets, unlike Jack, who confessed he has a mountain of debt. I wonder what I'll find at his apartment besides a room full of sneakers. It feels like it will be worth my while to dig into his files.

The cool air blowing in reminds me of when our group went in high school to Cedar Island. We rode our bikes on the ferry and ended up at an old resort. No one was around. Jack pushed on a door to an A-frame, and it opened. We went inside and found a set of stairs leading down to jail cells with bars.

The air was dank and smelled of mold. Rodent droppings dotted the cement floor. I shivered and said, "Let's get out of here. It smells bad."

My friend Abby rubbed her arms. "Yeah, this place is creepy and cold."

Buzz stepped inside a prison cell and inspected writing etched into stone. He pointed to the wall. "A guy was trapped here for a hundred days. Wonder how he got out?"

Jack, ever the joker, slammed the metal cell door shut with a clang. He chuckled. "Okay, Professor, see if you can get out. You're the smart one."

Buzz tried to open the door, but it didn't budge. Sweat formed on his upper lip. His face flushed, and a vein pulsed on his forehead. He stood back and crossed his arms. "Okay, jackass Jack, let me out. This is not funny."

Craig said, "I'll have no part of this." He and Abby left, their footsteps fading as they tromped upstairs.

Jack laughed, and the eerie sound echoed against the stone walls. Hairs on my arms stood on end. My breathing was shallow. My heart thumped. Buzz was trapped, and Jack was an idiot.

Buzz's face was beet red, and he rattled the bars. "Let me out."

Jack threw back his head and cackled.

I looked around for a key but didn't see one. I said, "I have to get above ground."

Buzz gazed into my eyes. "Don't leave me locked in. That would be cruel."

Jack, who was my boyfriend at the time, tugged at my arm. "Come on, let's go."

I yanked my arm away and reached for the cold metal door knob. Turning it, I threw the cell door open, and Buzz hurried out.

I hugged Buzz, and Jack said, "There you go, buddy. Free at last."

Buzz wiped sweat from his brow. "I won't forget what you did, Jacko."

Ever since that day, I've sensed Buzz resented Jack for the practical joke that made him panic. When we were eating pizza later on, the two exchanged a scowl. In that brief moment, they looked like they hated each other.

Now, I shrug. I went out with Jack because he asked me first. I was too shy to go up to Buzz and ask him to the movies. What would my life have been like if I'd asked Buzz before Jack said he'd like to take me to the dance? I'll never know. Choices were made, and paths were not taken. But what I'm sure of is my daughter is my everything, the one I run home to. She makes everything worth it.

I glance in the bathroom mirror. The night light by the sink casts shadows on a haggard woman. It hasn't been a day since Jack went missing, but I'm a hollow shell of myself.

I go down the hall to check on Kelly. She is on her side, her arms around the dog, and breathing softly. I kiss her cheek. She smells like baby powder and bubble gum. She wakes and says, "Did you find Dad?"

The dog opens his eyes.

I pat her shoulder. "Not yet. Go back to sleep. We'll find him."

She and the dog sigh and close their eyes. I climb in bed and drift off, dreaming of a night rescue at sea, where I am pulling Jack out of the water. I wake when I hear the toilet flush. Buzz comes to bed and slips between the sheets. His breathing slows.

I wait five minutes and stare into the dark. I'm wide awake, so I might as well leave the house early. Buzz snores softly as I pull on my clothes. In the kitchen, I hastily write a note. "Got to go. Love you both. Be back when I can."

21

I drive to Jack's apartment at four-thirty in the morning. The fuel dock isn't open yet, so I might as well inspect his place now. The air is damp and cold, making me shiver. My back muscles tense. No one is out, not even the dog walkers. My tires hum on the pavement.

If I find Jack alive, I'll give him a harsh reprimand for scaring us because of his bullheaded refusal to wear a life vest. If only he'd followed Craig's orders. Skippers have the final say. We should have left Jack on the dock, instead of heading out with a rebellious guest on board.

I pull up to his building, where he lives on the second-floor with a peek-a-boo view of the shipyard, and park on the street. I get out and zip up my fleece jacket. With the late September chill in the air, I need to get out my puffer jacket when I get home.

I climb a dim stairwell illuminated by a bare bulb. Jack didn't mind the missing caulk in the windows frames, or wind whistling on stormy nights in the old rooming house. He said it felt like home, and it cost less than most places. He wished he lived back in a time when digital devices weren't as important and at everyone's fingertips.

When we were going out in high school, he tossed a stick in the channel and gazed at a fishing boat going by. He said with a sigh, "I want to be a fisherman. But my parents are telling me I have to go to college and study engineering."

I frowned. He was a free spirit, not a math genius or careful sort of person who would measure twice. "What're they thinking? That doesn't fit you at all."

After high school off he went to a state school on the other side of the mountains for a semester but then he was back home, grinning about failing classes. I urged him to follow his dream when I saw him again. "Go fishing in Alaska. Do what you want. Follow your dreams."

But he never did. Instead, he stayed in town and resented his parents for pushing him in a direction that didn't suit him and anyone who liked what they did for work. Unfortunately, that included me, but I didn't realize it until after we were married.

One day I asked him to help me make the bed and cook dinner.

He said, "I've had a long day. You do it." He flopped on the sofa and turned on the TV.

I crossed my arms and tapped a toe. "I've had a long day, too, working on the boat. I'm exhausted. Come on, help me."

He glared and didn't budge. "Being a short-order cook is much harder than your job. You're doing what you always wanted. I'm working just to help pay rent."

I blew out a breath of frustration. "You could do something else if you dared. Don't blame me because I'm getting my hours to qualify for my captain's license."

He turned away and muttered in a sing-song voice that sounded like he was imitating me, "I'm working towards my captain's license. Big deal. But I can't lift a finger when I'm at home."

"Look, it's not easy for either of us now. We don't have enough money. But when I have my captain's license, I'll get better jobs, and I'll be paid more. We can move out of this dump into a better place."

The tenant above us stomped on the floor, and the ceiling light fixture trembled. The lights flickered. The man yelled, "Quiet down, I can hear you up here."

I said in a soft voice, "I bet we could save money and start a family."

My heart thudded as I waited for his reply, but I knew my timing stunk. Here we were arguing, and it was the worst time to bring up having a baby. We couldn't even make it through a night without picking at each other.

He stood from the sofa and wrapped his arms around me. "Sorry, I'll make it up to you. I'm just grumpy because everyone's getting ahead except me. It feels like my dream of making a lot of money will never come true."

I patted his back. "We don't need a lot of money to be happy. We need to appreciate what we have."

But we never got to that goal line. Sure, we had our baby girl, and she is our treasure. She's the best of us wrapped in innocence with a halo of hope. I want her to follow her dreams and be able to pay her bills. I'll teach her to find the joy in life, if I have to dig it out with a pick-axe. When things fell apart and we divorced, that hidden heap of happiness was elusive for many months. When I saved enough to buy a boat and start my own business, that brought a smile to my face. Kelly beamed the first time I took her out.

The steps creak as I go up to Jack's place. I doubt he defied death and is there, but I want to check. I pull out the key to his apartment.

22

———

I stop in front of Jack's apartment, Number Seven. Someone across the hall is snoring. It must be Mr. Abernathy, a retired tug boat captain. He falls asleep in his recliner in front of the television. I know this because I lived here when we were married. Most are long-term tenants, who stay for the reasonable rent and proximity to town, being a block from restaurants and a short walk to grocery stores and the library.

A mouse skitters past, and I bite my lip. Jack didn't want to use rat poison or mouse traps in the apartment with Kelly around. He has a good heart, but he lacks common-sense. That's what my mother said when he quit his short-order cook job to be a bartender, but then he refused to wear the uniform the hotel provided.

I wince about his job losses and vow to stop squabbling if he comes back. But I want him to pay me the overdue child support. I'll use the money to help Kelly take classes for whatever her dreams entail.

I wrinkle my nose at the odor of closed in cooking smells and insert the metal key into the hole. Jack complained his key didn't always work on the first try and required jiggling to gain access, so I'm not discouraged when I encounter resistance. I rattle the key in the lock and hope I don't wake the neighbors.

Somewhere in the building, a chair pushes back and scrapes the floor. I hold my breath. Jack could be on the other side of the door, alive and well. I hope he has fought back death and overcome obstacles.

I smile, reminded of how I have pushed past barriers at work. Some skippers didn't want me on their boats and said it was bad luck to have a woman in the wheelhouse. Others didn't want to sign off on my time sheets tracking my hours on the water. But I kept my eye on the goal of running my own business. I kept my mouth shut and put out fenders, pulled them in and stowed them in lockers on board, threw out the dock lines, and polished railings and stanchions until I could see my face reflected in the metal.

When the lock clicks open from the other side, my pulse picks up. I grasp the brass door knob, the metal cool in my hands, and turn the knob. The hinges creak as the door swings open.

My mouth falls open. The lights are on, and a man is

sitting at the dining table with his back to me. He shuffles through papers and then stands.

"Craig, what're you doing here? How did you get in?" I close the door and lock it.

He shrugs, shoves his hands in his pockets, and looks at the worn wooden floor boards. He has dark circles under his eyes. We've been friends for years, and I've never seen him like this. He shifts from side to side, like he is hiding something.

I have no idea what Craig is doing here, but my instinct is to protect Jack's place while he's gone. We all have secrets we'd rather not have people paw through. A million questions race through my mind. "What're you doing here?"

He rubs his chin, and I'm standing close enough that I hear the scratching sound of day-old stubble. "Well, you see, it was like this." He pauses.

I say, "You're acting strange. Cough it up, whatever it is."

He folds his arms and turns his back to the table. I get the feeling he is trying to block my view. "Why are you going through Jack's papers? I don't think he'd like this."

I glance outside. I don't have much time. The sun is rising, and two tall sash windows show a pink and blue sky. I push past Craig and scrutinize papers on the table.

I say, "You shouldn't be looking at his bank statements."

Glancing around, I take in the room. A drawer is open in an old beat-up desk. The wastebasket is upside down. Wadded up papers are strewn across the floor.

He clears his throat and cocks his head, as if he has every right to be here. His silence makes me suspicious. I never trusted Craig completely, not after the episode at Fir Island. I say, "It looks like you've been here for hours. Why did you come here?"

He grabs his coat and pulls it on. "I've got to go. Jack made me promise not to tell anyone. Melody is waiting for me at home."

"Who is Melody?"

He smiles. "My new girlfriend."

"You didn't bring her yesterday on the boat because?"

"Didn't want to put her under pressure. We just met the other day."

He starts for the door, but I block his way. "Does Jack owe you money?"

Craig frowns. "I wouldn't exactly put it that way."

"What did you get him involved in?"

He shakes his head and mutters, "Mind your own business."

My hands clench. "I'll find out. I won't give up."

Craig stares at a floorboard. The aroma of questionable activities wafts off Craig like a strong cologne. He moves toward the door. "See you around."

I say, "I hope you didn't drag him into something shady."

He yanks the door open and hurries down the stairs. I lock the door with shaking hands. Turning to Jack's paperwork, I search for clues about what he was up to and why Craig was interested in my ex-husband's finances.

23

───────

Jack's apartment is cold, and I shrug on one of his leather jackets. Sunrise sends slashes of pink, purple, blue, and red across the sky. I focus on the documents on the dining table.

Craig had a history of run-ins with the law. According to him, they were minor scrapes, where he was in the wrong place at the wrong time, and he was innocent. His wealthy family hired attorneys to bail him out of jail and get the charges reduced. When he was charged with running a scam, the lawyer convinced the judge Craig had nothing to do with it.

Now I wonder if there was more to the story. I could see him doing something illegal for the adrenaline rush. My friends share a tendency toward addictive behaviors. I'm hooked on the drama of rushing to help boats in distress. Jack collects sneakers and can't stop buying them. Buzz hoards books, and his house is packed with them. Abby is a clothes hound. Craig craves money and talks about getting richer.

I sink into a chair. Jack's disappearance is making me question everything I know about my friends. A niggling thought nags at the back of my mind. Buzz has talked with Craig and Jack by phone a bunch of times since he moved in with me. I tried listening from the next room but couldn't make out what was said. When he hung up the other day, I said, "What was that about? You sounded secretive, talking in a hushed voice."

Buzz shoved his hands in his pockets and shrugged. "Nothing."

If I didn't know him as well as I do, I'd suspect him of keeping something from me. But Buzz is a rock I can trust. Maybe he was making plans for my birthday. Last year, my friends threw me a surprise party on the beach for my fortieth, complete with a blazing bonfire and a guy who played guitar.

I pick up a bank statement and study the numbers. My eyes grow wide when I notice a deposit of ten thousand dollars. A week later, the same amount was transferred to another bank.

Slapping the paper down on the table, I say, "Where did you get this money? And why didn't you use it to pay me child support?"

Scrawled handwriting catches my attention. Jack

scribbled my boyfriend's name in the bank statement's margin and wrote, "Talk with Buzz."

I swallow hard. Does Buzz have something to do with Jack's money problems and the bank transfers and repeated deposits? I check the papers piled on the table and whistle at how Jack led a different financial life than I imagined. I hope Craig didn't drag Jack into trouble. Jack would be an easy target with his trusting attitude and his history of making impulsive decisions.

My phone rings, and I answer it. I'm on call when distress calls come in and other rescue operators don't reply. When the Coast Guard contacts me, I go out.

I say to the Coast Guard operator, "Sure, I'll take that. What's their number?"

I jot a phone number on a scrap of paper and hang up to call the skipper in distress.

"I lost power," the skipper says in a frantic voice. "We're drifting."

"What's your position?"

He says, "West of Skyline Marina in Rosario Strait."

I say, "I've got to get fuel first, but I'll be there as soon as I can."

I shove the paper in my pocket, flick off the overhead light, and head out, locking the door behind me. I hurry down the stairs and jump in my car.

Driving to the marina, a smile spreads across my face. There were nights when I was a kid alone in the apartment and the wind howled, rattling the windows. We didn't have enough money to keep a bedside light on while my mom was at work. More than anything, I wanted to be rescued from my situation. Now I'm rescuing others and being paid in the process. I get to roar across the water to help boaters. The little girl who cooked dinner for herself in a dingy apartment is the one who is taking care of others.

My mind goes to the skipper whose boat is adrift in Rosario Strait. Freighters and oil tankers ply those waters. Tugboats haul barges and log booms. My pulse picks up, and I park at the marina and hurry to my boat.

24

I stop at the fuel dock with my boat and put diesel in the two fuel tanks. I tell the young woman working at the counter, "Put it on my tab." She smiles and waves, and I depart.

Heading west through Cedar Channel, I scan the water and shoreline for a body washed up. I grip the steering wheel tight and vow to find out what Jack and Craig are involved in. Whatever it is, I suspect Jack's motivation was to own more sneakers.

I frown. If I had my way, I'd pay off his debts by selling the shoes and let Kelly use the spare bedroom when she stays there. But I'm not Jack. What a tangled mess he got himself into.

The engine rumbles as I go through Cedar Channel. An old wooden building on pilings that once held a cannery juts out into the channel. A tug boat passes, going the other way, and I wave. The captain waves back with a smile. We're bonded by our love of the sea and by making our living working on the water.

I come out into Rosario Strait and push on the throttle to increase my speed. Waves thump against the hull. I'm strapped in the seat, and my head is pushed back with the force of moving forward.

Up ahead, a sailboat drifts in the water. I slow my speed and hope this won't take long, because I want to search for Jack. He might be washed up on a rock, at the base of a cliff, or on a sandy shore. He is out there, and the sooner we find him, the better.

I approach the boat and hail the skipper.

He waves his arms. "We're drifting toward the shipping channel."

"Permission to board your boat, captain?"

"Permission granted. Just fix it, and I'll be on my way."

"I'll do my best."

I lash the boats together at midships and hop on the other boat, looking around. The seventy-something year-old skipper is weather-worn and looks like he's spent a lot of time exposed to the wind and sun. A man with him in his late seventies shuffles as he walks. Like the skipper, he looks like he knows his way around boats.

I say, "Tell me what happened."

The skipper says, "It felt like someone grabbed the boat from underneath. I lost steering and didn't have control of the boat." He rests a hand on his stomach.

"Did you see anything in the water before this happened? A yellow floating line?"

He shakes his head.

I say, "It might be a line wrapped around your prop. I'll tow you away from the shipping channel, put on my dive suit, and inspect your prop. If a line is wrapped around the prop, I'll cut it off, and you'll be on your way."

The skipper says, "Go ahead and get it done. I hope it'll be as easy as that."

"Before I proceed, I'll need your credit card for a deposit."

He hands it over, and I run it through a device attached to my phone. I hand him the card and say, "There you go. Let's see if we can wrap this up in no time."

He stuffs the card in his wallet. "Sounds good."

I point to a blue-hulled tanker coming up fast. "I'll move us out of the channel."

I step on my boat and put the engine in gear, towing the boat out of harm's way. The tanker chugs past, and I turn the wheel so our bows face a wave headed our way. Waves smack us, the boats bob up and down until the line of waves pass, leaving us in peace.

I open my tool kit and pull out my sharp knife. I've got to get this job done and be on my way. I have a lot of detective work to do before I pick Kelly up at school, and none of it was on my radar when I crept out of Buzz's house this morning. I want to ask Buzz if he knows what Craig and Jack are up to. Will he tell me the truth if he knows something? He'd better, because I trusted him with my daughter's heart. I wouldn't have let him get this close if he wasn't worth the risk.

I tug on my dry suit, strap on the tanks, put the regulator in my mouth and slip on my face mask. I slide the knife into a sheath on my diving belt. I wave to the men watching from the other boat and step into the sea. With each mission like this, I trust that my equipment will work. Each time I surface and climb my swim ladder, I send a word of thanks that I made it out of the water alive once more.

The water is cold, but it won't kill me with my protective layer. As I swim to the other boat, I think about Jack and how much he means to me. If he heard me say that, he would grin and say, "I guess you still care for old, loveable me. Why don't we get married again?"

I frown because if I am distracted, I could be swept away with the current and never be seen alive again. In the murky water, it is clear to me that if I don't pay attention, I could join Jack and end up a bloated, dead body drifting miles away.

Bubbles float past my eyes, heading to the surface. The sound of a boat passing whines in my ears. I swim to the propeller and turn on my headlamp.

25

Thick yellow polypropylene line is wrapped around the propeller. No wonder the skipper lost power. I pull out my knife and cut the line. When the prop is clear, I store my knife and swim to my boat, climbing the ladder to the swim step. I pull off my mask.

Inhaling briny air, I blow out a breath. One more job is in the books. I'm saving money when I can for if Kelly wants to attend community college or trade school. She'll have choices I never did, and I'll make sure I'm a better mother than I had.

The skipper runs a hand through his graying hair and says, "How'd it go?"

I hold up the yellow line. "This was wrapped around the prop, probably floating in the water. I'll get out of my suit and come over to your boat. Why don't you start the engine? I want to be sure you can make headway before I leave you."

I pull off my dry suit and hang it in a locker where water will drip down a drain. Kelly's new yellow rain jacket reminds me of how tall she is. My eyes mist over, and I wipe them with the back of my hand. I'm not ready for her to grow up. We're bound together, Kelly and me, but we'll part ways eventually so she can live her own life.

I step on the other boat and say, "Got her running?"

The skipper says, "Yep. I can go in forward and reverse now. Works fine."

We shake hands, and I hop on my boat, untying the midship lines binding us together. I move away and look back to make sure he is underway. The sailboat putters toward Cedar Channel.

I tour the west side of Fidalgo Island and look for Jack. All I see are rocky shores, sandy beaches, and driftwood logs. I slow down to better see a hidden cove on Burrows Island. Little waves lap the shoreline. With a sigh, I call Mike at the marina office.

I say, "Any news?"

He says, "The search continues. This is a tough time, looking for someone we know and like."

I swallow tears. "It sure is."

"I wanted to ask, why wasn't he wearing a personal floatation device?"

I sigh. "Jack wouldn't wear one. He said it was too bulky. But it was a thin inflatable vest."

I tug on my light-weight life vest with three snaps. What is odd is that on trips in the past, Jack wore one.

Mike says, "Vanity did him in? Wow."

I groan. "I know. He was wearing a blue Hawaiian shirt. Did anyone see it?"

"No. But his clothes could've been torn off by the waves."

I grimace and say, "I'll cover a wide area this morning. The chances of finding him alive are sinking with each second. See you later." I hang up and cruise along the north shore of Cedar Island. A few beach combers are out. I call Buzz to see how the school drop off went.

He answers and sounds upset. "She refused to go to school and said she wanted to find her dad. I tried to get her in the car, but she stomped off and said I wouldn't understand."

I smack my forehead. This is an emotional time for Kelly. Instead of supporting her, I left and went about my day on my own. We should have stayed together. Instead, I'm running around on a wild goose chase. Jack could be anywhere in these waters. His body might have been carried across the border into British Columbia, Canada and floating near Vancouver Island.

I'm about to head to the marina when I spot a patch of blue fabric drifting in the water by a floating log.

My heart thuds. "Buzz, I've got to go. I think I just found something."

"Call me back. Let me know what it is."

"I will. Bye."

I hang up and fix my eyes on a blue piece of fabric that might be Jack's shirt.

26

I stare at the floating blue fabric and bring the boat closer. It is partly my fault Jack went in the water without a life jacket. Craig sent me out on deck to make Jack wear it, and I should have carried out his request. Looking back, I see how casual I was about letting Jack be Jack and put himself in danger.

I cringe and wonder what I'll find. The current could have pulled off his clothing when he was swept overboard. If Jack is bumping around under this log, I will have no choice but to greet a cold dead body in the gray water. He can't have survived this long.

I put the engine in neutral, and the boat glides alongside the log. A body might be caught in a tangle of brown bullwhip kelp wrapped around the log. I don't want the propeller hitting it.

An eerie stillness settles over the misty gray water. A

seagull cries. The sound of a siren in Millersville comes across the water. A wispy white cloud rises from a hill on Cedar Island.

I inhale a deep breath of briny air and turn to my unpleasant task, reaching out and touching the slick round log. I move the log along until I come to a blue Hawaiian shirt with orange and purple flowers. It looks like the shirt Jack was wearing yesterday.

I squint at two nails, which are driven into the shirt, attaching it to the wood. I've never seen anything like this. I tug on the shirt, and it tears as I rip it off the log and bring it onto my boat. On this quiet morning, the moment is surreal and saturated with weirdness. This can't be real. No one nails a shirt they wore to a log.

The shirt is sopping wet and smells of funky low tide and the mysteries of the deep unknowns at the bottom of the sea. I note my position to pass along to the Coast Guard and putter away, checking for other signs left behind by my former husband.

I slowly move away and stare at the shoreline for more signs of Jack. Nothing moves on a stony beach. Was he delusional, nailing a shirt to a log?

Maybe he was trying to tell us something. I pick up the shirt and examine it. On the inside of the collar, Jack's writing in black marker catches my eye. "Don't look for me. Love Jack"

I gasp and let the shirt drop to the floor. It settles into a soggy mound at my feet. I steer toward the marina and make a sour face, totally confused about what I found. This doesn't make sense. Of course he wants to be found. What he wrote is difficult to grasp and is giving me a splitting headache.

If he climbed out of the water, he would have shivered uncontrollably and lacked the strength to find a hammer and nails and affix his shirt to a log. He would have had bigger concerns, like finding shelter and getting warm. This must be his idea of a party trick, but I won't be played.

I grit my teeth. Given Jack's offbeat sense of humor, I could see him doing this, perhaps as a practical joke. He'd be the center of attention, which is how he likes it. If he engineered this and it backfired, he's a bigger fool than I thought. You don't dare death in the face and expect to come out alive. The sea doesn't make special allowances or cut deals for jokers. The roiling water takes its toll.

27

I call over the marine radio and ask to talk to the Coast Guard commander in charge of the search. The Coast Guard says they'll call me back in fifteen minutes. I call Mike at the marina and say, "I found something, but you won't believe it."

"What is it?" he says.

My phone buzzes with an incoming call from the Coast Guard commander. I tell Mike I'll talk to him later and answer the call. "I'm searching for Jack Fishbone, who went missing overboard yesterday, and I found something of his near Cedar Island."

She says, "What did you find?"

"I found the shirt he was wearing when he fell overboard. The strange thing is, it was nailed to a floating log and there was writing inside the collar."

She says, "What is the location where you found the shirt? Can you provide the coordinates?"

I give the location where the log was drifting. "The writing inside the collar says not to look for him and he signed it. I know his signature."

She grunts. "Are you sure it was his shirt?"

"Pretty much. I'm almost one-hundred percent sure."

"We plan to suspend the active search tomorrow."

I frown. Kelly will be sad to hear that. We can't give up on finding her father.

She says, "Turn the shirt into the Millersville Marina office, and we'll send someone to pick it up."

I glance at the wet shirt. "Can I have it back later on? We might want it to remember him by."

"Sure, just leave your name and number with the shirt at the marina office. In the meantime, we'll send a vessel out to patrol the area where you found it. Send me photos of the shirt and the writing on it too. I'll examine it, but this could be a hoax. A search like this can bring out the crazies."

She says her email address, and I jot it down. When she hangs up, I take a few pictures and email them to her. I also send them to Mike and Buzz.

I decide not to send the photos to Craig. Something about how he acted in Jack's apartment this morning before dawn, like he had something to hide, makes me want to withhold information from my friend until I know more about what he was up to. I have a sneaking suspicion he wants to cause trouble and bury Jack under a pile of whatever plan he set in motion.

Going thirty miles an hour, I fly over the water while keeping an eye out for Jack's body in the water. He might not want to be found, but I won't stop looking for him. He won't get away easy or pull off the great escape. I'll track him down if it's the last thing I do.

28

———————

I back the boat into the marina slip, tie up to the dock, and stride to the office with the shirt and to tell Mike what I found. I'm not sure if fingerprints or DNA are detectable on clothing after sitting in salt water. But just in case, I lifted the shirt into a plastic bag with a pair of tongs. I'm trying my best not to ruin an investigation, if one starts.

Later today I'll go to the police and report Jack missing. The writing on the collar made it sound like he is hiding out somewhere, perhaps from debt collectors. But escaping doesn't sound like something a loving father would do. Jack wouldn't leave Kelly and abandon her. Or would he? One time he left town and didn't call or text or email to let me know where he was. My stomach churned with worry until I grilled Buzz and learned Jack was gambling at a casino near the ocean.

When I heard that, I took a tomato I was about to slice for a salad and squeezed it until it became a messy red pulp in my hand. Jack wasn't the best at making money decisions. When we were married, he bought a chainsaw and charged it on our credit card. But we lived in an apartment and had no use for a chainsaw. My eyes bulged when I saw the charge. I needed a part for my boat and the debt tore at my gut because of the way I grew up.

When I was little, my parents argued about my mom buying me a new dress or taking me to the hairdresser. My dad's voice rumbled low and harsh. He'd say, "You've got to control your spending. We're in debt over our heads."

But that ended when he was taken to prison and we ran off to start a new life.

When I learned Jack was gambling, I said to Buzz, "He told you where he was going, but he didn't tell me, his wife? I can't take it anymore. This is the last straw."

Buzz's eyes gleamed, and he almost smiled. But then he wiped a hand across his face and looked serious. "Are you sure you want to do that? It's a radical step, splitting up. You guys have been together a long time."

Buzz looked at me with his basset hound eyes, and I patted his shoulder to reassure him. "Don't worry. He's gone to sneaker head conventions so much lately, hawking his buttons that say, Sneaker Heads Rock, that Kelly and I will be fine. Not much will change."

Buzz said, "If you need anything, let me know. Just call or text, and I'll be there." He opened his arms, and I gave him a hug, the type friends from high school do when they greet each other after a long time. It was no big deal.

I filed for divorce, and Jack didn't seem surprised. I waited a few months, and kept my eyes open for someone who was the opposite of Jack. They had to be responsible with money, a hard worker, punctual, a rule follower and an all-round nice guy. I went out on a few dates and was disappointed, so I stayed home with Kelly or went out with our group of friends.

Jack and I shot daggers across the top of the wood grained table, but we were civil. Buzz and the others eyed us cautiously, watching for fireworks to explode. But we kept our tempers, especially when Kelly was with us.

Years after Jack and I split up, I was afraid I'd turn into a skeleton waiting for Mr. Right. And then one day, Buzz brought over flowers and asked me out. Our odd triangle of Jack, Buzz and me was cut down to the two of us, and it was a relief to hang out with an old friend who was becoming much more.

Now, as I hurry down the dock, a stiff breeze rattles the halyards and makes boat masts moan. Fingers of cold air creep under my collar, and hairs on the back of my neck stand on end. I shiver and zip up my jacket. I've got to drop my water-logged parcel with Mike in the office and get in touch with Buzz. I want to find out what Buzz knows, if anything, about the bizarre writing on the shirt. He's close to Jack and might know something.

The plastic bag crinkles with each step. I want Jack

found dead or alive because Kelly needs closure. I bite my lower lip and mull over what the writing on the collar said. It's possible that Jack wrote it, and he doesn't want to be found. But what kind of man would be cruel enough to leave his daughter? Despite his faults, I have a hard time believing he'd do that to Kelly. It would cripple her emotionally. Her grades would fall. She'd never get over it.

The marina office comes into view. The lights are on inside, and Mike stands at the front desk. I wave to him, and the bag with the wet shirt bumps against my knee. Mike might not believe what I'm about to tell him. Buzz might not buy into it and find it too far-fetched. It does sounds out there. If I told the tale to other boaters at The Brown Lantern, my favorite hang-out, I'd be laughed out the door for telling tall tales.

I open the door to the marina office and plop the plastic bag on the counter in front of Mike.

He leans on his elbows and eyes it.

I say, "The Coast Guard is sending someone to pick this up."

He cocks his head. "Okay."

"I was looking for Jack and found this shirt nailed to a log. It looks like the one he was wearing when we fell off Craig's boat yesterday."

Mike's eyebrows shoot up. "How could it have gotten nailed to a log? Maybe it's someone's idea of a practical joke?"

I squish up my face. "There's handwriting inside the

collar, and it looks like his. What if he wrote something there before he was swept overboard? Maybe he planned to get away, and this was his desperate plea."

Mike nods. "I guess it could happen, someone disappearing to escape debt. We play poker together Wednesday nights, and he's been on a losing streak."

I rub my temples. Although Jack might run from bill collectors, he wouldn't ditch his daughter. I brush a tear from my eye. The man I married would never abandon his child, but Jack has changed, and he owes a lot of money. Maybe I didn't know him, like I thought I did. I wonder what else I'll uncover as I dig deeper into his secret life.

29

A wall clock in the marina office ticks toward eleven. A microwave in the back beeps, and the smell of a breakfast sandwich makes my stomach growl. I want to grab something to eat and call Buzz. Mike cocks his head, looking at me with concern.

I say, "I've got to go. Give the shirt to the Coast Guard when they get here?"

Mike says, "I will. You said the shirt was nailed to a log in the water? I've never heard of anything like that before. This beats all."

I nod to him. Ever since I stepped off Craig's boat onto Fir Island yesterday, my world has gone wonky. Details and doubts swirl in my mind. Nothing makes sense. I doubt Jack is alive and hiding. That is not his style. He likes to be seen and the center of attention.

I rub my eyes. "It's almost like Jack planned to disappear, or this is someone's idea of a sick joke. You and I know his odds of surviving this long are almost non-existent."

We share a grimace and grow silent. I cast my mind to supporting Kelly in the coming days. It will take her years to recover from losing her father, if she ever does. She'll carry the wound forever.

Finding a body will give us closure. But like trying to grasp a white wispy cloud, our efforts may amount to nothing. We might never know where his final remains rest. Crabs could be nibbling and consuming his flesh right now, as I stand here. His body might be washed up on the shore of a remote island. Possibilities run through my head, each with a devastating impact on my daughter.

Mike taps the counter. "It definitely doesn't look good."

"The Coast Guard said they're planning to suspend the active search tomorrow. We'll be lucky to recover the body at this point. It could've drifted to Canada."

He says, "I agree, but we won't tell Kelly that. She needs to hold out hope for as long as she can."

I yawn and cover my mouth, nodding. He knows Kelly because we've stopped in for years. I'd tell him about a deadhead off D dock, and he'd call maintenance to get the hazard out of the waterway. Or we'd jaw about the weather and the cold front coming down from the north. Kelly wanted to go along, instead of my calling a neighbor to babysit her, when I answered distress calls after school and on weekends.

I say, "You're right. We won't tell her. And for all we know, a fisherman passing by might've plucked Jack from the water. He could be getting warm by a roaring fire."

He tilts his head. "Not likely, but possible. I'll give you that."

I hold up an index finger. "The writing on the collar is suspicious. What if someone faked Jack's death?"

Mike says, "I've worked here for twenty years and seen my share of strange happenings. But this tops all I've seen or heard until now. Give Kelly my best, and I'm sorry she's going through this. It must be tough."

He opens the plastic bag with the shirt and peeks inside.

I say, "You can look but don't touch it. Maybe the police can get evidence off it. What if someone forced Jack to write that, or they faked Jack's writing. It's a long shot, but just in case."

Mike closes the bag. "You take care."

"You too." He looks like he has something he's not saying, so I say, "What is it?"

He scratches his beard. Like many men in town, he has a trimmed gray beard and wears a flannel shirt and jeans. "Jack told me he had an easy way to make money and did I want in?"

I whoosh out a breath. "I hope he didn't drag you into something."

"Nope, I wasn't interested. I'm saving my money for retirement and can't risk it."

I grip the edge of the counter. "Did he tell you what it was? How did it work?"

"He wouldn't say." His eyes open wide. "Do you think he took people's money?"

I clench a fist. "I don't know, but it might not have been above board."

He flinches. "Something strange is going on."

I nod and grasp the metal door handle. "I agree. The pieces don't add up." I open the door and step out into a cool breeze. Jack's disappearance has put him in the spotlight, surrounded by chaos, just how he likes it.

I stride to the car, climb in, and call Buzz. I've got to eat, and I need help figuring this out. Karina's warm scones are calling my name. My mouth waters as I call Buzz.

He answers on the second ring. He owns the used bookstore, and the place sounds packed with people talking. An espresso machine's whine pierces the air.

He says, "What's up?"

"Meet me at Gigi's Café, okay? I'm starving and strange stuff is happening. I want to run it by you and see what you think."

He lowers his voice and the background noise grows quieter, as if he's stepped away from the front counter. "I can't leave. Matilda called in sick. It's her little girl again."

I chew on my lip. "That's too bad."

He muffles the phone, and I hear someone say she'll fill in while he steps away. He gets back on the line. "Okay, I'll meet you at the café. Grab a table if you get there first. But away from the door, because I hate the draft that comes in."

I snort. "How long have we known each other? A gazillion years? I know that about you." Considering how he is cooped up all day in the store, I add, "The wind is kicking up, so wear a jacket."

He chuckles. "Thanks, Mom. I want to hear all about what you found."

Recalling how his name was scrawled in the margin of Jack's bank statement, I say, "And I have some questions for you."

"See you there."

30

I park down the street from the café and hurry past cars lining the street. The influx of new people moving here when they retire hasn't led to a crime wave, but they do make my favorite place for quiche and scones more crowded. My stomach rumbles with hunger.

In our small town, if a person needs help, we chip in however we can. People say hi on the street, even to strangers. Kids don't avert their eyes but smile and say hi when they pass by. It's a slice of small-town America, and pinch me, I live here.

Gigi's Café is located in an old two-story house. A big tree out front casts a shadow, and the branches are close enough to claw at the tall sash windows. The previous owner passed away and willed it to her granddaughter, who was working as an artist in Seattle. Karina gave up her dream to keep a deathbed promise to her grandmother, who raised her, but now she looks happy to be running the cafe. Despite being on her feet and baking all day, she smiles when bringing cups of coffee and food to customers.

I walk in the door and spot a two-top open in the corner. I wave to Karina, the new owner, and make my way to the table. She wipes her hands on her flowered apron worn over brown leather pants. A tiny diamond stud in her nose sparkles, and her hair is bright pink.

Bets, one of the bartenders at The Brown Lantern, and her husband, Zerk, slide into the seats I was aiming for. Doesn't that beat all. This is just like the day I had yesterday, where everything went wrong.

Bets wiggles her fingers at me in a wave, and I return the gesture. She mixes a mean drink, and so does Zerk, and they can make me laugh, but there's something mysterious about them. I can't quite put a finger on it.

Bells on the door jingle, and I turn to see who came in. Buzz nods to me and scans the place, and I do the same. Every table is taken. I let out a sigh, and rest a hand on my growling stomach. I don't want to get take out and sit outside at the picnic table. After being on the boat and finding the shirt, I want to sit inside and be warm and waited on.

Karina comes over and rests a hand on my shoulder. "You almost nabbed the two-top, didn't you? If you weren't so friendly, saying hello to me, you would've gotten there first."

Bets waves us over. "Hey, we took your seats. Come join us. Grab two more chairs and squeeze in. We want to hear how the search is going,"

Zerk fingers the dragon tattoo on his neck. "Absolutely, we shouldn't have scooted ahead like that while you were distracted. You're working hard on the water, and we took the chair out from under you. Come on, I'll find two more chairs and bring them over. All right?"

I shrug. "Sure, I don't see why not. Thanks."

Buzz says, "Thanks. I can't take long. I've got to get back to the store." He and Zerk bring over two folding chairs from the back.

Buzz and I drink coffee with Bets and Zerk and order slices of quiche and fresh-baked scones. I sigh with contentment, and my tense back muscles start to relax. Sitting in a warm cafe with friends is a welcome relief after being chilled on the water. I warm my hands by clutching the white porcelain mug and inhale the rich, nutty aroma of roasted coffee.

Buzz turns to me and says, "What did you find this morning?"

I clutch the cup. "It'll take a while to explain. Some weird stuff is going on, and maybe you guys can help me sort it out. Or the police can when the station opens again."

Bets and Zerk look worried when I mention the police, but then they look at each other and laugh.

Bets tilts her head. "The police station is closed weekends."

Zerk smiles. "Because we all know that criminals take weekends off."

We laugh, but Buzz, serious as ever, says, "They still have two patrol cars making the rounds on weekends. That doesn't stop."

I kiss his cheek. "We're safe in Mayberry, for now." I don't say it, but I think, 'Until Jack comes back, tries to trick us into a scam, and his debtors shake him down.' It wouldn't be right to smear his name in front of Bets and Zerk until I have a firm grasp of the facts. Besides, Zerk is known where he works as having a tendency to spread gossip.

Zerk raps a hairy knuckle on the table. "The whole town is talking about how you and Jack fell overboard and he is missing. But you're making it sound like there's more to this story than a possible drowning."

Bets says, "By the way, we were very sorry to hear that Jack is missing."

Zerk nods. "He's a great guy, the life of the party. People light up when he walks in at the Lantern, buying drinks for people sitting near him."

I roll my eyes. Great, the guy doesn't pay me his part for his daughter's care, but he's buying drinks at a bar with abandon.

Bets nudges Zerk. "Hon, it's not the Lantern, no one calls it that except you. Everyone calls it the Brown."

He grins. "It doesn't matter, sweet love of my life. What matters is we are living another day in paradise. This is the best place on earth."

Buzz slaps the table with an open palm. "That's right."

I lean in, glance around to be sure mothers of Kelly's friends aren't within listening range, and say, "Before I tell you what I found, I need your absolute vow that this will go no further. We have to keep this between us. I don't want it to spread like wildfire. If people knew what I'm about to tell you, they'd blab it all over town."

Bets and Zerk look at each other. She says, "We get the need for secrecy. You can count on us to keep our traps shut. We'll zip it and forget it. Don't worry about us."

I chew on my lower lip, because I'm worried about these two. They are gossip central and they work at the hub of town, where everyone gathers to hoist a tall one. Or in my case, a glass of red wine. Make it a malbec, please. Silence settles over the four of us.

Buzz holds my hand with his warm one. He has the largest handspan of any person I've ever known. Sometimes I sit and stare at them, like they're birds about to take flight. Bigger hands mean the better for picking up books.

He says, "I promise not to say anything. Come on, spill the story. We're dying to hear what you found, and I've got to head back to work pretty soon."

Karina sets down four plates loaded with quiche and scones. "Enjoy!"

My mouth waters. The lightly-browned scone gives off a buttery smell. I put a paper napkin on my lap and reach for my scone.

Zerk says, "Could we get more coffee, please, and extra butter?"

"You bet." Karina rushes away as if she's in a running race, which I suppose she is, running this packed place during lunch time. She quickly returns with Zerk's butter and refills our cups with hot coffee.

I bite into a warm scone, take a sip of water, and say to Karina, who picks up my cup to refill it, "This is so good."

"I have more in the kitchen if you'd like to take some home to Kelly."

I smile. "I'll take two to go."

Bets leans across the table. "So, tell us, what is going on?"

I blow out a breath. "I was checking the area around Cedar Island after sunrise this morning."

Zerk says, "You were up that early? I was looking for my gold nail clippers, and you were searching for Jack?"

I shrug. "I couldn't sleep, and I had to go help a boat in distress. I'll tell the story, but don't ask questions until I'm done, or we'll never get through it."

The three of them nod, and I notice Karina hovering at the next table. But I go ahead and explain about Craig being at Jack's place and his going through the bank statements, and my fixing the sailboat engine.

Zerk says, "You're handy, being able to fix engines. I admire people who can do that. How did you learn?"

"I went to diesel mechanic school."

Bets elbows her husband and shushes him. "We promised to be quiet. Let her talk."

Buzz says, "Go on, Irena."

Karina moves away with the coffee pot and goes in the kitchen. I wonder how much she heard, and if she'll tell anyone about Craig looking over the papers. I hope not. Gossip could ruin Craig's reputation, and I don't want that on my shoulders. His insurance agency clients might drop him, and he'd have to sell his boat.

Jack's disappearance is disrupting our placid lives. Everything was fine before he was swept overboard. I feel a flash of guilt that I survived and climbed back on the boat but he didn't, and I brush it away.

I shift in my seat. When I surfaced, I didn't think about helping Jack. I was solely focused on my own survival in the frigid water. My only thought was to save myself and get on the boat. And for that, I'll never forgive myself.

31

I glance around the café to be sure no one is listening and say to Buzz, Bets and Zerk, "I need to find out why Craig was at Jack's going over his financial papers. But something else happened this morning too."

Bets says, "From experience, I can tell you it isn't good when someone is in an apartment going over papers." She shakes her head, as if it is an ill omen.

Zerk checks his fingernails, which look like he just had a manicure. "She's right. What you said about Craig being there is highly suspicious. You should watch him. Keep an eye on him twenty-four-seven." He points two fingers at my eyes and back to his.

I say, "I've got to sleep. I can't follow him around all the time."

Zerk says, "We can help. We have expertise in monitoring potential criminal activity, as long as you don't mention it beyond this table. We can put ourselves in their shoes and anticipate what a criminal is thinking. That's our secret skill, isn't it, Toots?"

He grins at Bets, and she leans against him and smiles. "We do, hon, we do. But let's not brag about it too much. We can't talk about our past."

I say, "It might be premature, but yeah, please keep an eye on Craig now and then, but don't let him see you."

Bets and Zerk beam, as if I've given them the gift of trusting them and bringing them into the inner circle as we hunt down the facts.

"We owe it to Kelly," I say, "to get a clear idea of what Jack was involved in. If there's fraud going on, I want to flush it out."

Zerk crosses his arms. "Don't you mean flesh, not flush it out?"

I smile. "I guess I mean both."

We chuckle. The tension of the situation is getting to us. Coming here, people were talking on the sidewalk in groups of two or three and casting furtive looks at me, speaking in hushed tones. They were absorbed, I bet, in speculation. Where was Jack? Was he alive or dead?

A draft drifts past, and I shudder, rubbing my arms. Poor Kelly, I hope she's not surrounded by swirls of speculation. The faster we resolve this and find Jack's body, the better it will be. I'd rather find him alive sitting by a fisherman's fire in a shack, but after this amount of time, the odds are against him having a beating heart. I'm glad we didn't find Jack's body last night when Kelly and I were searching. The image of touching her dad's dead body would have stayed with her forever.

I look them in the eyes and say, "Don't tell anyone about my finding Craig at Jack's place. Not a word."

Bets says, "We'll keep it on the down low, don't worry."

Zerk nods. "Discretion is our middle name."

They snicker and bump shoulders like kids goofing around. Buzz and I smile, but then I remember how serious the situation is. Someone might be dead, and the man was my husband. He's the father of my child. If he lost his life because he was vain about wearing a life jacket, I'll kill him.

I clear my throat. "I think I found Jack's shirt, the one he was wearing yesterday when he fell overboard.

Buzz blurts out in a loud voice, "You found his shirt?" His jaw tenses.

I say in a quiet voice, "I didn't want anyone else to know, not yet."

The café quiets. A hush falls over the boisterous crowd. I suppress a groan. It's as if I uttered the secret open sesame words. Everyone in the room is frozen, forks in mid-air, waiting for what they'll hear next.

At a table next to ours, a woman in a pink track suit says to her friend, "What doesn't she want anyone to know?"

Her friend, Shawna, who is about my age and in book

group with Ms. Pink, says in a loud whisper, "Something about a shirt. Be quiet so I can hear what she's saying."

Ms. Pink says, "We shouldn't eavesdrop."

People murmur. A buzz grows as questions fly around the room, bouncing off walls.

Buzz says, "I'll be right back, just need to use the restroom."

His chair scrapes on the wood floor boards. Bets and Zerk focus on eating. I shove bites of quiche into my mouth and swallow.

My pulse pounds in my ears. I've got a lot to do, and I need to find Kelly on top of it all. I want to know why Craig was in Jack's apartment, and I need to file a missing person's report with the police. I'd rather do that without my daughter listening to every word.

Shawna says at the next table, "Her ex-husband is missing, and I heard she was out looking for him. How romantic is that?"

Ms. Pink says, "I hope we learn something we can tell the book group."

I nibble at my scone. The coffee is warm, and I've lost interest in my food. Jack's disappearance has turned off my taste buds. I wish we could go back one day and start over.

Bets sets her fork on her empty plate and leans on her elbows. "It must be tough on your daughter, with her dad missing."

I nod. "It is. I hope we find him soon."

Zerk brushes tears from his eyes. "Poor kid."

Bets wraps her arms around him and gives him a hug.

Their tenderness about my child makes me wonder if they wanted a baby, but it didn't work out. I keep my mouth shut and don't ask. It wouldn't be right to ask them about kids. Everyone deserves to keep their private wounds away from prying eyes.

I glance around, wondering what is taking Buzz so long, and see him by the cash register, talking with Karina and Violet, who runs Outrigger Services. He sees me looking and holds up an index finger. The three of them huddle together. I wonder what they're discussing but then realize it has to be about Jack. That's all anyone in town is talking about today.

Moments later, Buzz slides into his seat and plants a kiss on my lips. He smells of a citrus aftershave and coffee breath. His clothes give off the odor of old books and espresso. I reach for his hand and hold it.

Buzz says, "Karina couldn't help but overhear part of what you said. Violet, her half-sister, recommends you tell everyone here all at once about the shirt. Otherwise, they'll make up stories. Rumors will spread and spin out of control. This way, people won't stop by your place to ask for details or be as likely to call or text and bother you."

Bets arches her eyebrows. "It's an unusual approach."

Zerk nods. "But maybe the best one, given how people love to talk in this town."

32

I sigh and study the café. I've been awake for a long time, and it is only midday. The tables are full. The mood is tense. Utensils scrape on plates. After I said I found the shirt, and Buzz blurted out his remark, I've felt eyes weighing on me, invisibly tugging and willing for me to spill the secret.

My former high school science teacher, Mr. Frackus, brings out a tray of warm scones from the kitchen. He sets them down on the front counter, shoves his hands in his apron pockets, and shoots me a quick look. Others stare. I know them, having grown up here. We've shared worries about friends and neighbors lost at sea, from sinking fishing boats, flipped over kayaks, and flooded canoes.

It feels like we're all holding our breath, while we wait to hear what I'm going to say, if anything. I nod to Karina and Violet, standing at the front counter and say to Buzz,

Bets and Zerk, "I might as well tell them and get it over with. It'll be easier that way. But keep what I told you about Jack's place to yourselves."

They nod.

I stand to address the room. My intention is to relay the facts and nip twisted gossip in the bud. But the one detail I won't share is that Craig was in Jacks' apartment examining his bank statements. I'll keep that part of my morning out of the rumor mill and hope Bets, Zerk and Buzz can keep their mouths closed.

I give Buzz a quick glance. I'll have a word with him later, because he's been known to run off his mouth, and we can't have that. Reputations are at risk, including mine. If I am accused of making false accusations, my business will tank. People need to be able to trust me with their vessels and their lives.

Looking around the café, I say, "Hi, everyone."

People nod. No one smiles. Mr. Frackus fiddles with his dark-rimmed glasses.

"Today is a sad day. As you may have heard, Jack Fishbone was swept overboard yesterday. We haven't found him yet, and the Coast Guard is searching."

Bill Rafferty, who owns a pawn shop and several other businesses, is sitting by the window with a muscled man in his thirties named Flash. He raises a hand and says, "Weren't you swept overboard too? Why were you able to make it back and he didn't?"

I gulp. "That's the big question, with one obvious

answer. I was wearing a life vest, and Jack wasn't. He refused to put one on and said it wouldn't look good."

People grumble. Bill Rafferty shakes his head and says something in a low voice to Flash.

I open my hands for emphasis. "Let's remember this as a lesson. Boating is a life and death activity. Jack was ready for a party and didn't expect to be swept overboard. The sea offers joy, but it can turn on us. We have a duty to our loved ones to be prepared for the worst."

Karina bites her lip and looks at the floor. Violet does the same, mirroring her body language, probably without knowing. They recently discovered they are half-sisters, and they seem close. Having grown up as an only child, I'm envious of their easy friendship and when I see them greet each other with a hug.

Violet says, "What about the shirt you found?"

I glance around the room. All eyes are on me. Fingers tap tables. The tension in the room is palpable.

"When I was out in my boat looking for Jack this morning, I came upon a log in the water on the north-east side of Cedar Island. The shirt was nailed to a log."

A gasp ripples around the room.

I say, "The blue shirt with bright flowers looks just like the one Jack wore before he fell overboard."

I take a slug of lukewarm coffee and keep going. Karina lifts the coffee pot, pointing to it, but I wave her off. I've had enough caffeine. Recent events have jangled my nerves. I'm a fuse in a stick of dynamite.

I hold up two fingers. "Two nails fastened the shirt to a log in the water. It's not just strange, I'd say it's bizarre."

Everyone nods.

"Not only that," I say, "someone wrote inside the collar, and it looked like Jack's writing. The Coast Guard is examining the shirt, but the writing said not to look for him, and he signed his name."

Karina claps a hand to her mouth. "No."

Her over-sized reaction makes me wonder what's going on with her. Is she the secret new girlfriend Jack mentioned but wouldn't dish out details about her? Or is the recent death of her grandmother bringing up feelings of grief?

Bill Rafferty's face pales. He leans over, whispers to Flash, and slaps money on the table. They walk out the door. I cock my head at their exit but decide not to read anything into it. They probably had to attend a meeting with a client. But come to think about it, Jack owes money to someone. He borrowed it and was over his head in debt. He might owe money to the pawn broker.

Karina puts her hands over her eyes, making me wonder how well she knew Jack. She seems awfully upset about him being missing. My suspicions are on high alert, and I suspect everyone of doing mischief after Craig's devious behavior this morning.

People turn to each other and talk. A din fills the room. The wood floor planks amplify the sound.

I say, "The Coast Guard is looking for him. But they

plan to downgrade the search tomorrow if they don't find him by then." I wipe a tear from my eye and clear my throat. "If you see anything suspicious, please call me, and let the police know. I'd like to know if someone forced Jack to write that or faked his writing. The whole thing has me upset. But please don't mention it to my daughter if you see her. She's worried enough as it is."

People nod and go back to finishing their meals.

Karina says, "Thanks for telling us what happened."

I sit and stare at my stone-cold scone and the remains of my slice of quiche.

Violet rests a hand on my shoulder. I flinch because I didn't see her come over. She is quiet as a cat, gliding along with ease. She's ex-military, so that might be where she learned to approach with stealth.

She says to Buzz and me, "So sorry to hear about your friend. It can't be easy on you. If you want help looking into it, like the hand writing on the shirt and all that, I have resources I can call on. Just let me know."

I say, "Thank you, I appreciate the offer."

She says, "Do you have photos of the writing on the collar?"

I nod.

"Send them to me," she says. "I'll take a look."

I hand her my phone, and she types in her phone number.

She walks away, and Buzz says, "Take a few more bites

of your food, babe. You must be hungry. Or we can get Karina to box it up."

"I'm not hungry. The whole thing is upsetting. I don't want to take it with me."

He urges me to eat more a second time, and I eye him with surprise. He wasn't this pushy when we were friends. Only after he moved in did he start acting controlling with a dose of caring. Will he become a controlling partner, and do I want to hang around and find out? I'll hold off on making major decisions until life settles down. This has been a very long morning, and my knees ache as if I've been carrying a heavy weight on my back.

Bets stands. "We'll keep our eyes open and let you know what we find. Don't worry about us blabbing." She elbows her husband. "Right, hon?"

Zerk gets up. "Right. We'll be in touch."

Something about the look she gave him worries me. Did I trust the wrong people? I don't want word getting out that Craig was pawing through Jack's financial information.

Zerk says, "You never know, we might overhear something that will be useful."

"Thanks for helping," I say.

Bets takes his arm and pulls him toward the cash register to pay.

I scoot my chair closer to Buzz and rest my head on his shoulder. He wraps his arms around me, and I lean into his warmth. I wish I could hide here forever, but I can't.

My head snaps up. "Where's Kelly? You said she didn't go to school?"

He says, "I followed her in my car and she got in and went into school. She's okay."

I let out a sigh of relief. Jack's mess is tangling up our life. I've got to follow the trail, which means going back and searching Jack's apartment.

33

Karina rings us up at Gigi's Café. Her eyes are watery, and she stops to blow her nose.

I hand her my credit card and say, "You're taking the news about Jack hard."

She nods and tosses the tissue in the trash. "Yeah, I am. The subject of death hits me at unexpected times, you know? Plus, he was a really nice guy. He came in here all the time."

I tilt my head. "How well did you know him? He mentioned he had a new girlfriend, but he wouldn't say who it was. He said it was too early to tell."

She bites her lip. "We're just friends."

Buzz shifts from side to side with his hands in his pockets, looking uncomfortable. There is a twenty-year age gap between Karina and Jack. I probably shouldn't have been rude and probed about them going out.

Mr. Frackus bustles past, carrying a gray plastic tray for bussing tables. He clears tables with an efficiency that fits with the science teacher I knew in high school. There was no messing around in his class. He ruled with an iron hand. It amazes me that he is helping Karina at Gigi's Café, but I guess he was a close friend of her grandmother's. Karina's younger cousin flitted off to a better job than part-time waitressing, so she needs the help.

Shane appears out of the back and takes off his apron. "Dishwasher is loaded. Want me to help people check out?"

Karina turns to her former high school boyfriend with a smile. "Thanks, I have a million things to do in the kitchen. Have at it."

He says, "I can only stay another half hour. I've got class and can't miss it."

Small town gossip spreads fast, and I heard Karina's cousin was going out with Shane, who is older and attending college. But I guess Lydia broke it off. There's a current of tension with an undertone of potential love interest between Karina and Shane. But as far as I can tell, nothing is happening yet.

Karina says to him, "I'll finish with Irena and Buzz, then you can take over." She looks at me and says, "Would you like a receipt?"

A line of customers forms behind us. They talk in loud voices and shuffle their feet. The front door is open, and a breeze blows in. Now that the big reveal about Jack's shirt is over, people are ready to pay and get on with their days.

I shake my head. If Jack is dead, Karina would be a role model for my daughter, as someone who is grieving a loved one's death and getting on with life. "No need."

Karina says, "Thanks for coming in. See you next time."

She goes in the kitchen, and Buzz and I head for the door.

Mr. Rasmus, the head librarian, stops us and says, "I'm sorry to hear about Jack."

I say, "Thanks. We're devastated."

We move on, and Ms. Pink reaches out and grasps my hand, holding on like it is a life ring. "I hope he's somewhere warm and dry."

I clear my throat. The news about Jack is a reminder about the other side of the curtain of life. Death is tapping a toe, waiting for us. We could be the next person to have a mishap. Jack lived as if there would always be another tomorrow. But what if today is all we have? I mull that over and say to Ms. Pink, "I hope so too."

By the time Buzz and I burst outside into the cool breeze, I'm wrung out and ready to scour Jack's place for clues. Deep within, if he is dead, I have unfinished business. Do I still love Jack? I must, because tears are streaming down my cheeks. I wipe them away.

Buzz stares and looks perplexed as we walk to my car. I

stop and say, "I'm pretty sure it's normal to cry about my ex going missing. He's a good friend and Kelly's dad."

Buzz pats my arm. "For a moment, you looked like you still loved him. A lot."

I sniff and tell a bold-faced lie. "I love him as a friend. I was married to him, and we had a child. It doesn't compare to what I feel for you."

He crosses his arms and stands with his feet apart. I tap my toe. Our relationship has turned chilly, like the cool wind blowing. Will our love survive Jack's disappearance? I'm not sure if it can. The stress might break our new bond.

He says, "I've got to go,"

I say, "A quick question first about Jack."

He shoves his hands in his jacket and purses his lips.

"I found a bank statement of Jack's in his apartment, and your name was written on it. Why would he have done that?"

He frowns. "I have no idea, and I suggest you drop this. You're not a detective, and it's a waste of time. Pay more attention to Kelly, given what she's going through, instead of running around trying to find your ex-husband and dig up facts about him. It's all you can talk about and becoming an obsession for you."

My mouth drops open. This is a new side of Buzz I haven't seen before, and I don't like it. I'm in charge of my life. He isn't. Who is he to tell me what to do? I have part of the puzzle about Jack's financial affairs, and I want to unravel what he was up to. If I went missing, I'd want someone to look into what I left behind. This is what friends do for friends.

Buzz says, "See you later." He hurries down the sidewalk, passing under thick branches stretching out from the tall tree outside the café.

I glance at his back and get in my car. I love two men, my ex, and my boyfriend. Is it possible to be in a relationship with Buzz while my love for Jack hovers in the background? I can see how that could undermine what I want with Buzz. By this time next week, Buzz and I will either be washed up on the rocks, along with Jack's body, or we'll sail into the sunset together. We're at a breaking point, and I have no idea which way it will go.

34

———

I hop in my car and stop at the police station before picking Kelly up at school. At the front counter of the police station, I say, "I'd like to report someone missing."

The officer says, "How long have they been missing?"

"Since yesterday afternoon."

She shakes her head. "I'm sorry, but that's not long enough for us to take a report. It has to be two days at minimum. Otherwise, we'd be wasting resources, running around looking for someone who took a day or two away from home. Maybe they needed a break and they're on their way back right now."

I frown. "I understand that's your policy, but this is different. He fell overboard. A wave washed him into the water."

She puts her hands on her hips. "If it happened on the

water, it doesn't concern the police. The Coast Guard handles that. Have you called the Coast Guard?"

My heart races. I release a slow breath and unfurl my clenched hands. I want her to file a missing person's report and blowing up won't help my cause. But in my mind, I'd like to shake her and yell. A man I loved is missing. We must do everything we can to get him back. Instead, I say, "We put out a Mayday call, and the Coast Guard is searching for him."

She tilts her head. "Was he wearing a personal floatation device? Just curious is all. My cousin's husband fell off a boat, but he was fine. The life jacket saved his life."

I blow out a breath. "Jack wasn't wearing one."

Her eyes narrow. "Why not?"

I shrug. "Because he's stubborn? Because he's a rebel and refuses to do what other people ask him to do? Because he wanted to look his best for our party that didn't turn out to be a party? But just because he made a bad decision doesn't mean we shouldn't look for him."

She taps a pen to her lips. "I'm sorry, but we'll have to wait the required two days to report him missing. That's our policy and we can't vary from procedures."

I rest a hand on the counter. "If he doesn't turn up dead or alive by tomorrow, I'll be back. And I hope you'll take this seriously then."

"We will, and we share your concern. I hope you find him long before then."

Her attention turns to a stack of paperwork on her

desk, and I take my cue and leave. That was a big waste of time. I gnaw on my lower lip. I need to go to Jack's and look around, but I don't have time before school ends. I'll take Kelly with me to search his place.

Outside, a stiff breeze blows past. I hope a boater in distress call won't come in before I comb through Jack's belongings for clues to what he was up to with Craig. The wind is picking up, and we're in for a storm. The barometer was dropping this morning. In weather like this, more boats run into rocks and put holes in their hulls.

I drive to school just as classes are ending. Clumps of kids wander down sidewalks, and I search for my daughter in the mix. I spot her, hips swaying and striding along, heading in the direction of our house. Unlike the others, she is alone. She is talented, and I admire her athleticism and creativity, and for finding an activity that gives her joy.

I pull up next to her and roll down the window. "Let's go to your dad's place."

She gives me a surprised look and jumps in the car. "Why Dad's? I was going to our house."

I pull away from the curb. "Something is bothering me, and we need to go through his things. I'll be honest with you. He may have been involved in questionable financial activity. And there's a small chance he planned to fall overboard."

She stares at me. "That's crazy. He wouldn't do that. He wouldn't leave us."

"I know, and I agree. But there's some strange stuff going on. I'll tell you about it at your dad's. It's better if you hear it from me anyway."

"I'm hungry. Can we get Thai food? Noodles would be good."

I shake my head. "We don't have time. With this weather, I might get a distress call, and I'll have to go rescue them."

She sighs. "I hate that you're always rushing out to help others. Can't you hang around home like a normal mother for once?"

I turn into the drive through of a Mexican restaurant. "I wish I could. But I've got to work. What do you want? Tacos?"

"Yeah, with extra sauce."

Five minutes later, I drive away with warm food in bags making my mouth water. Being with my daughter is a balm for my troubled soul, and I remind myself that she needs me now more than ever. I've got to be in service with her and let her talk about her feelings. Listen to her, I tell myself. Don't dominate the conversation.

Soon, we're thumping up the stairs, and I unlock Jack's apartment. My mouth falls open. I stop in my tracks, and the food bags fall to the floor. Kelly bumps into me.

She says, "Why is it so messy? Dad doesn't keep it like this."

Papers are strewn around the room. It is not like I left

it this morning. I groan and set down my purse, rubbing my temples where a headache throbs.

I say, "This happened after I left early this morning. Somebody came in here and did this. They must have been searching for something."

I don't tell my daughter, but Craig might have come back to find whatever he was looking for. Or if Jack owed Bill Rafferty money, he and Flash, his side kick, might have barged in and turned the place over, searching for money. My mind churns with ideas. I don't have answers, I have only questions perched on my shoulders like ravens, cawing in my ears, telling me to find Jack and the reason he or someone wrote in the shirt collar and nailed it to a log.

I cast a side glance at Kelly. What if Jack was secretly in despair because he was deep in debt? That happens to people. They cover it up. He could have been down in the dumps, but even his best friends didn't notice. I don't know Jack as well as I used to, but Kelly might have a clue.

"Did your dad seem down lately, like something was bothering him?"

She's quiet for a beat. "Yeah, he wasn't as fun. I'd come home and find him sitting on the couch writing in a note-book. But when I got close and tried to see what it was, he hid it. He wouldn't tell me what he was doing, but I could tell he was writing a bunch of numbers. He was using the calculator on his iPad, but when I looked over his shoul-der, he hit clear, and all I saw was it was a big number."

I rub my cheek. This could be the amount Jack owes. "How big a number was it? In the thousands, maybe?"

She shakes her head.

In a tight voice, I say, "Millions?"

She shrugs. "I think so. Maybe one or two million? Something like that. I didn't get a good look."

I whoosh out a breath and look around the room. Pillows are ripped. Couch cushions are split open. The TV is smashed. Papers are scattered. A file drawer hangs open.

I say, "Why don't you sit and eat while I call the police and report a break-in?"

She sighs. "I don't feel safe here without dad, not with someone breaking in."

I wrap my arms around her and give her a hug. "There's no one here now. I'll protect you. We'll stick together like a two-pack of sourdough bread loaves."

She giggles, and I wipe away the tears running down her cheeks.

Looking into her hazel eyes, I say, "I promise you we will get through this. Somehow, some way, we're going to come out the other side. We'll be stronger for it."

Her lips quiver. "I hope so." She sobs, and her shoulders shudder, and I hold her tight. I pat her back and make soothing sounds.

My phone buzzes in my pocket with a text, but I ignore it. My daughter is more important. A moment later, my phone rings before going to voice mail.

Kelly steps away and wipes her nose with the back of her hand. "You should see who it was. It might be an emergency and a boater in distress needs you."

I shrug. "I guess they'll have to find someone else to help, won't they?"

She cocks her head at this new, perplexing side of me.

The phone rings again, and she pulls it out of my pocket, answering for me.

"Rescue boat services, how can I help you?"

She listens and hands the phone to me, whispering, "You should take this call."

"Hello? Yes, this is she. What can I do for you?"

"My powerboat is taking on water. We hit a rock. Can you get here right away?"

I eye Kelly and say, "I'm sorry, but I have another situation I'm attending to. You'll have to find someone else."

"Please," the skipper says. "Help us."

The law of boating comes to my mind. I can't decline helping a boater in distress. It wouldn't be right, even though I want to stay here and call the police to report a break in. I won't knowingly ignore a boater in distress. Even though I'm not in my boat, I feel the pull of doing the right thing telling me to save lives and rescue boaters on the Salish Sea. If only I could have saved Jack yesterday and brought him back to the boat.

Kelly motions to me in the background, waving her hands and pointing to her chest. She mouths, "I'll go with you."

I say, "Tell you what, we'll be right there. Give me your position, and we'll race to my boat."

I hang up and hear a noise in the bedroom. It sounded like a door closing. I hold up an index finger to Kelly and put it against my lips in a sign to be quiet. Then I run down the hall and pull open the closet door, pushing back shirts on hangers. No one is there. My heart pounds as I check under the bed, finding dust balls.

Kelly joins me in the bedroom.

I point to a partly opened window and whisper, "What if someone climbed in?"

She says in a low voice, "Dad keeps it that way, says he likes fresh air."

I nod. "That's right, he does. I'll check the bathroom in case someone is in there. You stay here."

I creep out of the room. A flash of white catches my eye. Someone runs out of the bathroom and down the hall, feet pounding on the wood floor. The entry door slams shut.

Goosebumps prick my flesh. My heart pounds as if I've run a race. I rush to the door and lock it, then run to the bathroom and throw back the shower curtain in case someone else is hiding there. No one is there.

My hands are shaking. My knees tremble. I hurry to the bedroom to check on my daughter.

She is sitting on the bed, her head cradled in her hands. "Someone was here, weren't they? Did you get a good look at them?"

I sit by her and put an arm around her. "All I saw was a flash of white. The footsteps were heavy, so it might've been a big person or someone wearing boots."

She looks at me with wide eyes. "What're we going to do?"

I pat her leg and stand. "We're going to get out there and help that boater. And I'm going to call Buzz and ask him to come over and keep the place safe. He can call the police and report the break in."

We grab the food to go, and I call Buzz from the car.

He answers on the first ring. "Does this mean we're getting along?"

"Definitely," I say, checking to see if Kelly is listening. She stares straight ahead, but I feel as if every ounce of her being is focused on what we're saying. She told me last month she likes Buzz because he treats her like an adult.

"Listen, I can't talk long. Kelly and I are going on a rescue call. We were just at Jack's, and someone had been there. The cushions were slashed, and files thrown around, like they were looking for something. While we were there, someone came out of the bathroom and ran out, but I didn't get a good look at them. Can you go guard the place and call the police to report a break-in while we're on the boat?"

He says, "I don't have a key to Jack's place. He took it away last week when we had an argument."

I clench my jaw, frustrated that my plans are thwarted.

"We have a lot to talk about later. What was your argument with Jack about?"

"It was private."

I say, "You could sit in front of his door and guard it, so no one goes in."

"I have a bookstore to run," he says. "Besides, what would I use to defend the place? A stack of books?"

Kelly snorts and chuckles.

I roll my eyes, pull into the marina lot, and park. "We've got to go. Talk to you later."

35

Kelly and I jump out, slamming the car doors. We hustle down the dock to my boat, shrug on life vests, and I start the engine while Kelly stows the take-out food. When the engine is warmed up, Kelly pulls in the dock lines and the fenders like a pro while I steer the boat into deeper waters.

We buckle into our seats, and outside the marina, I floor it and head to the boater in distress. He is in the area off Cedar Island where I found Jack's shirt. I shake my head at the oddity of finding a shirt nailed to a log. An idea goes flitting by, and it occurs to me that all this drama might be a ruse orchestrated by Jack to be in the spotlight. I could see him raising money after this and taking donations to get out of debt. But I don't mention my wild speculations to Kelly.

I call the skipper and let him know we're five minutes away.

"Thank goodness," he says. "There's an inch of water in the boat."

"Be right there." I hang up and say to Kelly, "An inch of water isn't much."

When the boat is in sight, I slow down and tell Kelly, "Go ahead and eat."

She pulls a protein bar from her jacket. "I brought this. It'll do for now."

I glance at her. "Do you know what your dad and Buzz were arguing about? It's not like your dad to make Buzz give his key back. They're best friends."

She swallows a bite and says, "I don't know. I came home from school and heard yelling. When I opened the door, Buzz and Dad went quiet. Their faces were red. Buzz left, and Dad wouldn't talk about it when I asked what happened."

I thought I knew my friends, but in the last day I've learned everyone is carrying secrets. And some people are better at hiding them than others. "While we're out here, keep an eye out for your dad. He might be clinging to a log. You never know."

She tucks the wrapper in her pocket. "I have been. So far, no signs of him. Is the Coast Guard still searching?"

"They should be."

I pat the pocket on my cargo pants, where I tucked

Jack's most recent bank account statement. The paper crinkles. I took it this morning after Craig stomped out. With a yawn, I wonder what the person was looking for at Jack's apartment. I hope I'll find clues when I study the pages.

A low flying plane buzzes overhead, and a Coast Guard helicopter hovers in the area where I found the shirt attached to the floating log.

I point. "There's the Coast Guard."

She says in a quiet voice, "I hope they find him soon. I need to ask him something."

"What's that?"

She shrugs. "Just something that struck me as odd the night before he disappeared. I'll tell you about it later."

"Come on, don't make me wait," I say as we approach the boat taking on water.

"He was whispering on his phone when I went through the room. All I heard was something about meet me there. Do you have the money?" She gives me a wide-eyed look. "Strange, huh?"

"Weirder and weirder."

The boat crests a wave. Salt water splashes up, splattering the windshield. Two-foot white caps dot the water. The sea is angry and stirred up by a twenty-knot wind. The marine forecast this morning predicted a storm. We'll fix the boat in distress and tuck inside, back on land.

I say, "Time to put out the fenders and get the lines ready."

I slow the boat's speed to three knots. Kelly sets out

the fenders, and I come alongside the other boat. I hail the skipper with my hands cupped and tie up to the other boat at midships.

The two bound boats bob in the rough chop. I step across the frothing water onto the other boat, and my phone dings with a message, but I ignore it. Setting my tool kit down on the aft deck, I go into the cabin, where the skipper is at the helm. Water sloshes in the bilge. My job is to fix this and exit or tow the boat to a shipyard. I'm trained to do that, but I'd rather avoid the hassle and get the boat underway on its own power.

The skipper's hands are shaking. "Can you fix it? I couldn't leave the helm to check. I figured it was best if I kept going. That way, less water would come in and fill up the boat."

I don't argue with the man or get into a discussion. He has a point. If you have a gash in your boat, at times it is best to stay underway, stuff cushions into the gap, and pump out water until you can get help.

He's wearing a life jacket, so points to him for being prepared. I take his payment and say, "I'll look at your through-hull fittings and intake valves. One of them might've come loose. Have you checked them recently?"

He tugs on an ear lobe. "A through-hull valve? Never heard of it. What is it?"

"Not parts you normally see, but they're important." A wave smacks the boat, and I grab a handhold as we rock back and forth. "Hold on, I'll go check."

The wind is picking up outside. My pulse quickens. I want to get back to land, look into what happened to Jack and learn why his apartment was trashed. I pull up a hatch and look down into the bilge, where water is sloshing around. The bilge pump whines. The smell of diesel fills my nostrils. Although there is water in the bilge, it is not enough to worry me. I suspect the problem is elsewhere.

I hurry to the head, or the bathroom. The floor is wet and the floor drain is overflowing. I yank the cupboard door under the sink open, check the valve and tighten it with a wrench. I'm surprised the skipper didn't notice this, but people panic. When we're in shock, we can't see past our toes.

I straighten up and wonder if I am missing something obvious about Jack's clandestine activities with Craig. When I get to shore, I'll contact the police about the break-in, and I'll search Jack's place for the notebook Kelly mentioned.

The skipper leans in and says, "Is that what caused the leak?"

I brush my hands off on my damp pants. I should have changed into overalls before I came aboard his boat, but this was urgent, and he couldn't wait. I pat the pocket with Jack's bank statement. It is still there but a bit damp.

I say, "It certainly looks like it."

I make my way to the aft deck and store the wrench in my tool kit. In the last day, I've learned new facets about my friends. They aren't who I thought they were. I suspect Jack and Craig are involved in sketchy financial dealings. Buzz could also be involved.

I say to the skipper, "If I were you, I'd head to the marina and take shelter. A storm is blowing in, and it'll get rough."

We shake hands and say goodbye. As I maneuver my boat away from his, I say to Kelly, "How about we look for your dad before heading back?"

The light in her eyes tells me all I need to know. She says, "One last look before it gets dark. He could be waiting for us to find him."

She picks up the binoculars, scanning the water and Cedar Island.

I tell her about finding the shirt, the writing on the collar, and how the Coast Guard has it. She says, "It doesn't make sense. He'd come back to me, wouldn't he? He wouldn't leave me. He'd want to be found."

I swallow the lump in my throat. She'll be devastated if Jack doesn't turn up. "He would, I'm sure of it."

She says, "Everything was going so well. He just got paid a bunch of money, and he took me out to dinner at Nona's to celebrate. He was going to introduce me to his new girlfriend."

A twinge of jealousy plucks at my heart. I force my voice to sound neutral when I say, "Do you know who it is? The girlfriend?"

She frowns. "He was keeping it a secret until the right time."

My phone rings, and I put the helm on autopilot to answer it.

The Coast Guard commander says, "We've found something. We'd like to board your boat and show it to you. Our cutter is in the area and will deploy a rigid inflatable dinghy."

Adrenaline courses through my body. I grip the phone and say, "We'll hold our position off Cedar Island."

"They'll be there in ten minutes."

I hang up and say to Kelly, "They found something."

36

I slow our speed, and while we wait for the Coast Guard to arrive, we watch for Jack.

I say, "Eat the take-out food. You must be hungry."

Kelly holds up the binoculars. "I lost my appetite. I'm too worried." She points and says, "Here they come."

A rigid inflatable is headed our way with three people on board in orange life vests. Waves splash up. The wind moans and batters the boat. The weather is as dismal as we're feeling.

I say, "I know this is hard on you. I wish we could go back to the way it was, when everything was normal."

She snorts. "Nothing was ever normal between you and Dad. You both have big personalities, and it was like living in a TV show. You were acting a part for the other parent and competing for my affection."

I grimace. She caught me out and saw through us. "I wish we could've stayed together," I say, "and lived under one roof. It would've been easier on you."

She rolls her eyes. "No, you don't. You hate the way he spends money on sneakers he never uses. You fight all the time, and it would be worse if you were married. I'd rather you live apart. It makes for less drama."

I study her profile. Her chin isn't quivering. Her breathing is calm. She is telling the truth. Finding Craig at Jack's place has made me suspicious. I wonder if I'll trust anyone after this.

I squeeze her shoulder. "Thanks for telling me. I'm open to hearing whatever you want to say. Don't hold anything back."

She looks me in the eye. "I'd like to go to Seattle after high school to study dance."

I gulp and take a moment to recover. In a tight voice, I say, "If that's what you want instead of staying in town, I understand. You have to make your own way in the world. I'll do whatever I can to help you follow your dreams."

I stare at the approaching Coast Guard dinghy. Kelly can't leave town. I need her by my side. I'm not ready to let her fly away on her own. I hoped she'd work with me and take over my company one day. What she says makes sense, but I'm swamped with emotions I must cover up.

Rain pelts the windshield, and I turn on the wipers.

She points to the rigid inflatable boat. "I wonder what they'll say about Dad?"

A wave smacks the boat, and it rocks back and forth.

"I'm not sure, but we're about to find out."

I put the engine in neutral, shrug on my rain jacket and pull on a wool hat. Kelly does the same. I say, "Let's greet them and take their lines."

We head out into the wind and rain. My cheeks are wet, and I suspect the moisture isn't only from precipitation. I want to cling to Kelly and tell her to stay with me and keep me company forever. But I bite my cheek and am silent as the dinghy comes alongside with a thin-faced woman and two men, all wearing dark clothes under their orange life vests.

They lash the boat to mine, making quick work of it, and step over the choppy sea onto my boat. I usher them into the cabin, and we gather round, standing with our arms crossed. Kelly cocks her head, waiting to hear what they'll say. A blond man's cheeks are ruddy from being out in the wind. A slim Black man holds a clipboard and stands tall. The woman has a stern look, and she appears to be in charge. She glances around the boat and nods, perhaps conducting a quick inspection.

She pulls a zip-lock gallon-size plastic bag out of her pocket. "We'd like to show you an item we found to see if you recognize it."

I cringe and wonder what it will be. A wristband? Fabric from his shorts?

I say, "Go ahead, I hope we can help you."

Kelly's eyes grow wide.

The woman sets the bag on the navigation table, and Kelly and I lean in, inspecting the contents. It looks like the front part of a flip flop. "Does this look like something Jack Fishbone was wearing the last time you saw him?"

I look over at my daughter, and we nod. I say, "He was wearing black flip flops like that on the boat yesterday, even though he knew our friend likes people on his boat to wear white-soled shoes."

Kelly eyes the remnant of the flip flop. "He always wears flip flops, even though he collects sneakers."

The blond man snorts. His boss eyes him and purses her lips. He blushes and grows silent. The tall man jots down something on his clipboard.

She says, "That's all we need for now. Thank you for your assistance. We'll be in touch if we need more information. You found his shirt in this area earlier today?"

"I did."

She cocks her head and stares. "It was unusual, you finding it that way, when you just happened to be in the area looking for him. And the fact that the shirt was nailed to a log?" She shakes her head. "That's a new one for us."

I hold up my hands. "For me too. I've never heard of anything like that."

The cabin air almost crackles with tension emanating from her. She's chasing a lead and filled with purpose, and I admire that.

She says, "The handwriting in the collar was suspicious. It doesn't add up."

"I agree. But it fits Jack and how he operates. He craves attention."

"Do you believe he would disappear and not want us looking for him?"

Kelly says, "I don't. My dad would never leave me."

I shrug. "Maybe someone else wrote it."

"But you said it looked like his writing?"

I nod. "It does. I don't understand any of this or what's going on."

She shoves the bag in her jacket and takes a last look around. "That's all for now. Thank you for your cooperation."

She exits and the two men follow in her wake. They expertly untie their lines and depart, revving it up when they're five or so boat lengths away. The dinghy flies over the waves.

Kelly and I go in the cabin and I put the boat in gear. "Let's take the food, and do a re-do at your dad's. I want to call the police about someone breaking in and going through his stuff. Ready to go back?"

She sighs. "Yeah."

Waves thump against the boat as we head for the marina. Whatever is going on is making a muddled mess in my mind. The clues I've found so far perplex me: A shirt on a log. Handwriting on the collar saying let him go. A bank statement with my boyfriend's name written in the margin. Someone broke into Jack's apartment. I'm seeking the safety of hard facts, but Jack left tracks of deceit behind.

I frown and seethe with anger at him for leaving chaos in his wake. For convoluted reasons, I feel obligated to my daughter to figure this out. If Jack is dead, or he left on purpose, we will want answers. When we search his apartment, I hope everything will start making sense.

37

Wind plays with Kelly's hair in the marina. I add a spring line to keep the boat snug near the dock. A storm is coming, and we'll be ready. The wind moans through boat masts. Burgees on bows flap back and forth in a frenzied flutter. We grab the food, pull our knit caps down over our ears, and head to the car.

As we hurry by the marina office, Mike stands at the counter and gestures for us to come in.

I say to Kelly, "We can't stay long. We've got a lot to do."

"Right," she says, matching me stride for stride.

Inside, the office is warm, and I pull off my cap. "What's up?"

He takes a look around the office and says in a low voice, "Someone called and reported seeing Jack."

My eyebrows shoot up, and I turn to Kelly. Her face is pale.

I say, "Where was he seen? Are they sure it was him? Is anyone checking it out?"

He scratches his cheek. "It was from a burner phone, and they didn't give their name. A woman said she saw him in the Pak 'N Pay lot. He was running to an RV parked in a dark part of the lot, away from other cars."

I purse my lips. "That doesn't make sense."

"I agree. It sounded like a prank call to me. Weirdos come out of the woodwork when someone is missing."

I say, "Thanks for telling us."

He cocks his head. "How are you two holding up?"

Kelly's lower lip trembles. "Okay, I guess, but we're going back to my dad's. What if someone breaks in again?"

I pat her back. "I can leave you at home if you like while I go. It won't take long."

Mike says, "Wait, what happened? Someone broke in to Jack's place?"

I nod. "And they ran out while we were there."

Mike says, "That is scary. Did you call the cops?"

"I will," I say. "I would've earlier, but we responded to a distress call."

Mike rolls his eyes. "That guy used to keep his boat in Tacoma, and every year, there were rescue calls for him. Always something going wrong."

I say, "Whoever broke in at Jack's was searching for

something. I need to file a police report and look around to see what's missing."

He says, "Kelly can stay with me while you do that. We'll have hot chocolate and watch the storm come in, like we used to. It'll be like old times."

I smile, despite anxiety churning in my gut. What will I do if the person who broke in comes back?

Kelly says, "Thanks, but I'll stay with my mom. I want to change clothes at Dad's place. Whoever was there was looking for something, and maybe I can help figure out what it was."

"Thanks, Mike," I say. "See you around."

We head outside, and I take my hat out of my pocket. But the bank statement I took from Jack's apartment falls out and blows away, pages skittering down the sidewalk.

I run after them and call to Kelly, "Help me get those back."

I snatch paper from the pavement. Kelly grabs a sheet, and I pick up the last page. We stop in our tracks, breathing hard. Her cheeks are rosy, and there's a light in her eyes. We have them all.

The challenge of reclaiming the papers gave us a small measure of success, but we have far to go. I want to sit and study what Jack has been up to and interrogate Craig and Buzz. I'd like to have a good talk with Buzz and dispel the underlying tension between us. Everyone is upset about Jack going missing, with tempers flaring at the slightest provocation. I'll have to watch myself with my daughter, because I don't want to take my frustrations out on her with harsh words.

I fold the pages and stuff them in my zippered inner jacket pocket, where they should have been stored all along. I shake my head at my carelessness for almost losing them, and we head to the car.

Kelly says, "What are those papers for? You acted like they were really important."

"They're your dad's last bank statement. I could've gotten it online, but I don't know his password. I want to figure out where he was getting money from and where it's going."

As I start the car and drive to Jack's, she says, "Dad's been different lately. I think something is bugging him. The other day he was whispering in the kitchen with Craig."

I glance at her. "What were they saying?"

"I don't know. They shut up as soon as I went to the frig. All I heard was something about investors and how they were going to make a lot of money."

I gnaw on my lip and wonder what is going on. I pat her knee, the one person I can count on. "Maybe we'll figure this out when we look through your dad's stuff."

She sighs and stares out the side window. "I hope so."

On the way, I think about calling Buzz but decide to put it off until after I call the police. By then, I'll have a better idea of when Kelly and I will be home. I'm not sure how I feel about him right now after our tense talk about Jack yesterday and our disagreement earlier today.

I pull over and park. Getting out, I hope Buzz and I can smooth over our feelings and go back to laughing together. Except this is not a time for joking. This situation is dead serious. I'm torqued out of shape about what he said, but I've known him for years, so I'll give him the benefit of the doubt before breaking it off. He is embedded into our lives and a big part of our friendship group, so I don't want to cast him aside for a few remarks. He sounded jealous of Jack, who isn't even here. We're in a circus and the ringleader, Jack, left, but we're still running around like clowns.

We slam the car doors, and I follow Kelly up the steps to the second floor. It was for her that I was in my boat looking for Jack this morning. And it wouldn't be right to leave the search all up to the Coast Guard, not with my fast boat and experience in rescue and recovery. I would have been negligent if I didn't take another look, and I couldn't live with that.

We hurry down the hall, and I hope we'll find answers and information about what Jack was involved in. I suspect Craig dragged him into a devious scheme, but I've seen Jack get into debt on his own for the right pair of sneakers.

Jack's door is ajar.

My heart thuds. I fling a hand out to hold my daughter back. Floor boards creak in the apartment.

Someone is moving around. What kind of menace waits inside?

My armpits prickle with sweat. I whisper, "Stay here and wait. I'll be right back. I'm fed up with people messing with your dad's stuff."

Kelly hisses. "Don't do that. Call the police."

I know she's right, but I slip inside, treading quietly.

38

───────

The intruder moves around with his back to me. If I didn't know better, I'd swear it was Buzz. He's wearing the same black T-shirt as when I saw him at Gigi's Café. He moves quickly around the room, running his hands under couch cushions. He bends down on his knees and peers under the couch.

A dull headache throbs in my temples. I clench my hands. He said Jack took his key back. Speaking to his broad back, I say, "What're you doing here?"

He pivots in place, and his eyebrows shoot up. His face turns bright red.

I cross my arms. "What are you looking for?"

When he doesn't answer, I call out, "Kelly, it's okay. You can come in."

Kelly steps in with a neighbor who is retired and lives across the hall.

Mr. Abernathy pushes back his gray hair worn in a comb over. "I let Buzz in because he's a friend of Jack's. I've seen him here many times, until they had a loud argument last week. I heard Jack went missing, and Buzz is looking for something to help us find Jack."

I nod. "Thanks, Mr. Abernathy. Good to see you again."

He turns to leave. "Just knock on my door and return the key when you leave. Jack always liked me to have an extra, in case he lost his."

Buzz says, "Thanks, I appreciate it. I'll stop by later."

I say to him, "What're you looking for? And did you call the police to report the break in, like I asked?"

He gives me a kiss on the lips. "I didn't think you were coming here."

I open my arms. "Well, here we are. Would you please tell me what's going on."

He folds his arms and eyes me, as if deciding how much to share.

Kelly says, "I'm going to change my clothes."

My hands clench. Why is it so difficult to get information out of my supposed friends? Maybe they aren't my friends after all, or they won't be when Jack's disappearance is settled.

I say, "What has Jack been up to? Are you involved in an illegal scheme with him?"

He holds up his hands. "That's far-fetched. I feel like

you're accusing me. I'm not here to steal anything. I got in with the help of a neighbor who knows me."

I slump into a seat at the table. "Then tell me everything you know. Kelly and I deserve answers."

He swallows, and his Adam's apple moves up and down, like it does when he's nervous. He is hiding what he knows from me, and I want to know what it is. Couples shouldn't keep secrets from each other. At least that's what I always thought until now.

Kelly opens the refrigerator. The frig hums. "Nothing in there now," she says. "Just some old orange juice and a nasty-looking old sweet potato."

I toss her the car keys. "Go out and get the take-out food. We forgot it in the car."

She catches the keys mid-air and leaves.

Buzz sits, wiping his hands on his jeans. "I didn't mean to confuse you by not telling you everything I know. I figured withholding information was better, so you didn't know the whole story about what Jack was doing. We blew up at each other, and he took the key back, when I told him I didn't agree with his approach."

I lean forward. "What was he doing that you didn't agree with?"

Kelly slides into a seat next to me and opens the white paper sack. The smell of Mexican food wafts out. She digs in while Buzz and I talk.

Buzz tilts his head. "You sure you want to hear this while Kelly is here?"

She says, "Please tell us. Get it over with."

I say, "She's old enough to know. It'll get out, eventually."

He clears his throat. "All right then. Jack got into a get-rich-quick scheme with Craig. They're printing fake stock certificates for shares in companies that have gone bankrupt and selling them over the phone to senior citizens, telling them when a big event is announced, the stocks will go up in value and be worth a lot. They're preying on people who live alone and don't have family or friends looking out for them."

He shakes his head. "I hated how they were targeting vulnerable older people. They found recent widows and widowers from obituaries and called them, figuring they'd be overwhelmed. They drove down streets and knocked on doors of houses with older cars out front and neglected yards. They went online and looked up property records for rundown houses, thinking the owners might be frail and unable to keep them up." He frowns. "They were thorough, it was wrong, and Jack was the one in charge."

My gut churns with acid. Our friends wouldn't run a scam targeting the elderly. I stare at the chipped table Jack bought at a garage sale for five bucks. I was the one who helped him carry it up the stairs. We were friends, despite splitting up, and we trusted each other.

I say, "That doesn't sound like the Jack I know. He doesn't like to work hard. He wouldn't be in charge."

Kelly says, "Mom, it's not very nice to talk about Dad

like that. We don't know this is true until it is proven. Right now, it's gossip and talk."

I break into a coughing fit. "He loves older people. I can't see him doing this."

Buzz squeezes my hand. "Craig put him in charge because he was sincere and could charm strangers and get them to trust him."

I nod. Jack is a charmer, that's true, and that's why I fell for him.

Tears stream down Kelly's cheeks. She says in a shaking voice, "Are you sure? Dad always tells me to be honest."

I let go of Buzz 's hand and pat her shoulder. "I agree. It runs counter to everything I've known about him. And I was married to the guy."

Buzz glances away, as if he doesn't need reminders of how my life is intertwined with Jack's. I sigh. If Jack is dead, I'll be a single parent. For years, I've enjoyed talking with him as a sounding board. We'd meet and make decisions about Kelly together. I'll miss that if he's gone.

I step into the silence. This is a lot to absorb, and I want to verify what Buzz said. Part of me refuses to believe Jack is a scammer.

I say, "Did you report him to the authorities?"

"I threatened to. That's what our argument was about. I said I'd turn them in if they didn't stop."

I drum my fingers on the table. Kelly gets up and grabs

a roll of paper towels from the counter, ripping one off and using it as a tissue. She blows her nose.

While I'm trying to wrap my mind around what Buzz said, he speaks up. "There was one other thing we argued about. And that was about me seeing you."

My brows furrow. "Why was that?"

"He said we shouldn't see each other. That he had a prior claim and if anyone should be dating you and taking you out, it would be him."

Kelly gets up. "I'm going to pack some things."

She grabs some clothes from a hamper by the bookcase, which is filled with cookbooks Jack collected but never used, and disappears into the bathroom.

I say, "It sounds ridiculous that Jack thought he'd have a say over who I see."

Buzz slouches back in his seat. "Yeah, same here. We got into a pissing match about it. I said some things I wish I hadn't."

"Like?"

He shrugs. "That he was an idiot for letting you go. That if he was better at keeping a job, you wouldn't have left. I said he should've treated you better."

I nod. "That's pretty much right."

He stands, and the chair scrapes as he pushes it back. "How about we go out to eat? I'm hungry."

I massage my tight jaw. "I lost my appetite when I heard what Jack was doing." A wild thought slips out of my mouth. "I don't want to leave in case Jack comes back.

And I want to go through his things. Something valuable must be here if someone broke in.

He rocks back on his heels. "Jack has got to be long gone by now."

I stand and lower my voice so Kelly won't hear. "Are you saying he's dead? Or he planned to disappear and he's hiding somewhere?"

Kelly comes in the room and stands by me. She says to Buzz, "Do you know where my dad is?"

39

Buzz runs a hand through his blond hair. "Last I knew, he was stashing cash in safe deposit boxes at banks. He wanted to take a trip to Mexico and hide money there. I don't know how he planned to get it across the border."

Kelly leans into me. My throat is tight with tears. Our lives revolve around Jack, and I can't imagine his taking off and abandoning us.

I say, "It sounds like you think he planned this. But a rogue wave washed us overboard. It was an accident."

He leans on the table, and it rocks. The legs never were the same length, which reminds me of how unstable the truth is. He says, "What if he planned to go overboard? But the rogue wave beat him to it, and he took advantage of it?"

I gasp. "But you're not sure?"

"No, I'm not."

Kelly says, "If you're not sure, I don't think you should be spreading rumors that make me sad."

I shoot Buzz a harsh look. "She's right."

He holds up his hands. "Guilty as charged. It just makes sense to me. Jack wanted money and lots of it. He was always talking around us guys about it and trying to come up with ways to bring in cash. But he didn't want to work hard for it."

I croak out a forced laugh. "Don't we all wish we had more money? That's perfectly normal. But I don't think he would've gone to those extremes."

Buzz says, "I hated not telling you what he was doing for money, but I was bound by secrecy."

I say, "You could've gone to the authorities to report it. Were you worried you'd be an accomplice and charged for a crime?"

His Adam's apple bobs up and down. He fingers the collar of his black t-shirt. "They made me promise not to tell. If I did, they'd mess with your boat. I care too much to let anything happen to you."

My jaw drops open. "They were going to do something to my boat?"

"Yep."

"Do you know what they had planned?"

He tugs on his T-shirt. "Something with the propellor?"

I splutter. My boat is how I make money to pay my

mortgage. "I'll turn them in. They can sit in jail and die for all I care."

Kelly looks at me. "I don't want Dad to go to jail."

I say, "What was Jack going to do with the money?"

Sweat forms on his upper lip, and he wipes it away. "He wanted to build a resort in Costa Rica."

I say, "But he's never even been to Costa Rica. Are you sure?"

"He wanted to live where he could wear shorts and flip flops all year long. Said he saw a show about it and decided to start over."

My eyes grow wide. An inkling of knowing taps at the back of my mind. Jack mentioned he wanted to move to a warmer climate, but I blew him off and said I was staying in our area for the boating. I didn't believe he'd follow through, not before Kelly was old enough to be on her own.

Kelly says, "Aren't I more important than money?"

"You are," I say, squeezing her shoulder. "But let's not jump to conclusions. We don't have all the facts."

"I think we have enough to go on," he says.

I let out a sigh. "It's hard to believe Jack would scam people and leave us."

Buzz 's jaw clenches. "You've got to trust me."

Kelly says, "My dad wouldn't go without me. I don't care what you say."

We're quiet for a moment, each lost in our thoughts.

Buzz says, "Want to head out for dinner?"

I glance at my daughter, who shakes her head ever so slightly. "We'll stay here a bit longer. We need time to absorb what you said, and I want to search the place."

His eyes well with tears but he blinks them away. "I was just telling the truth. You wanted to know, so I told you. It's not my fault. It's all Jack's doing."

I walk him to the door. "Don't stay up late on our account."

Buzz hurries away and thumps down the steps.

Mr. Abernathy opens his door. "What's the racket? Who's stomping down the stairs?"

I say, "Buzz, my boyfriend."

He cocks his head. "But you're with Jack."

"I was, but we've been divorced for years."

He says, "Doesn't seem that way to me. I heard you laughing in his apartment. Sounds carry in an old building like this. Didn't I see you leave at midnight last week?"

I eye a brown water stain on the ceiling from a busted pipe in the upstairs unit. While Kelly was at a sleepover, I had a few beers with Jack. "We hang out sometimes and talk about our daughter."

Kelly rolls her eyes. "They're always joking around."

Mr. Abernathy nods. "Any word on Jack?"

"Not yet." I say, "But please don't tell Buzz I was here late. He was out of town at a book convention, and he doesn't know. He's sensitive about that."

Mr. Abernathy raises an eyebrow. "Doesn't sound right to me."

Kelly says, "You always tell me secrets get you into trouble."

I cross my arms. They might be right. "Just don't tell him this time."

40

I close the apartment door and lock it. "I'll call the police and then order pizza. We've got to eat something, even though we're upset." I call the police.

She plucks a potato from the frig and slams the door shut. She drops it in my lap. "What is this?"

I say, "I'm on the phone. Hang on."

A dispatcher comes on the line, and I say, "I'd like to report a break in." When I describe what happened, she says, "An officer will call you back."

I hang up and pick up a hard plastic potato. "This was in the frig?"

Kelly says, "I've never seen it before."

Noticing a seam, I pry the plastic potato open.

Kelly peers over my shoulder. "What is it?"

A scrap of paper is inside. I pull it out and read a series of numbers. Swallowing hard, I stuff what I think is an account number for an offshore bank account in my pants pocket.

Kelly holds out her hand. "What is it? Show me. I'm not a kid. I need to know."

Shaking my head, I say, "Sorry, but some things you don't need to know."

She frowns and her hands fly up in the air. "I'm grown up. Let me see it."

I stride to the couch, where cushions are cut open and the stuffing is on the floor. "Someone came in looking for something. I have to keep you safe."

She holds out a hand. "Show me what you found."

"I'll order pizza while we wait for the police to call."

She says, "Do what you want. I'm not eating anything you order." She strides into the bedroom.

I call after her, "While you're in there, look for that notebook your dad had."

She slams the door.

I call and order a medium pepperoni pizza and a salad. She marches into the bathroom and shuts the door. When I hear the toilet flush, I wait a few minutes and knock on the door. "Everything all right in there?"

"No, and it never will be right. Not after I learned what I did today."

I lean my forehead against the doorjamb. "Maybe we'll find out it isn't true. I have a hard time believing your dad would rip off older people."

"It sounded real." She blows her nose.

I knock again. "Will you open the door?"

Before she does as I ask, someone knocks hard on the front door.

I hurry over and say through the closed door, "Who is it?"

"This is Officer Kendricks. You reported a break in?"

Kelly comes out and stands beside me as I open the door.

A clean-shaven officer with brown hair steps in and introduces himself. I gesture to the slashed pillows with stuffing torn out, the open file cabinet drawers, and papers thrown around the room.

He says, "Quite the mess. Is this your apartment?"

"No, it's my ex-husband's. But we're friends, and he gave me a key. This is our daughter, Kelly."

He nods. "When did the person or people come in, do you think?"

I examine the water-stained ceiling and mull over his question. So much has happened since Jack fell overboard, and the order of events is jumbled in my mind. "I'm not sure. I came by this morning, and a friend of ours was here. A file drawer was open and papers were on the table. I left around six-thirty in the morning. Whoever came in after that wrecked the place."

"Who was here in the morning? And what time did you come back?"

I purse my lips. Our relationships are burning down,

so I guess it doesn't matter if I name Craig. "It was our friend Craig, and he has an insurance company to run."

I run a finger across my chapped lips. I want to track Craig down, tell him off for roping Jack into a scheme, and verify what I heard. There is a chance Buzz embellished the story to make Jack look bad.

I clear my throat. "The last two days are a blur. I came back around four or five?"

Kelly says, "We got here around four-thirty, I think."

The officer examines the door. "Doesn't look like the lock was forced. How did they get in?"

Kelly says, "My dad gives his friends keys, so they could come in if he was running late, which happened a lot."

I nod. "They'd play poker and watch football."

The officer tugs on an earlobe. "Pretty tough to find the culprit if they're coming in using keys. It could've been one of his friends or a stranger who did this."

Kelly frowns. "Are you saying Craig did this?"

He says, "We don't know. Your mom says he was here, he had access, and he was looking for something." He turns to me. "Could your ex-husband have come back and done this?"

I shudder. "He wouldn't do that. He liked his things and wouldn't damage them."

Kelly tugs on a strand of hair. "Yeah, he wouldn't do that."

"Mind if I take a look around before I go? I'd like to see what the other rooms look like."

I gesture down the hall. "Go ahead."

The three of us go into the bedroom, where the mattress has been pushed onto the floor. The end table is turned over and a drawer pulled out, tossed in a corner. I pick up the drawer to slide it into the end table, and my fingers touch the underside.

I turn the drawer over. "What's this?"

41

I'm about to pull a taped piece of paper from the bottom of the drawer when the officer snaps on disposable gloves. He says, "Hold on. We don't want to tamper with evidence or destroy fingerprints."

He strides over and takes the drawer from me. I decide not to mention to the police officer the numbers on a slip of paper in the plastic potato in the refrigerator. I want to ask Craig and Buzz about it before turning it over to the police.

He says, "Whoever was here was looking for something. Do you know what they wanted to find?"

I say, "I have no idea."

Kelly scuffs a shoe on the matted-down beige carpet.

I turn to her and say, "Do you think they were after the notebook your dad kept?"

She shrugs. "Maybe. He was secretive about it. But I don't know where it is."

The officer says, "What did it look like?"

"He was always writing in it, but when I'd get close, he snapped it shut. It looked like a lot of numbers next to people's names. It was one of those school notebooks the size of a looseleaf piece of paper, and blue on the outside. He wrote in black marker on the cover, Jack's dreams. I wanted to find it but never did."

He says, "Was anyone in your group of friends jealous of Jack for any reason? That might amount to motivation for looking through his things. Maybe they were trying to find the notebook you mentioned."

I cock my head. "Most of us were upset with Jack because he didn't pick up the tab when it was his turn to pay and we all went out. But that wouldn't be big enough to make someone come in and trash his apartment. He was fun to be around and has a great sense of humor, so we still invited him along when we went out."

Kelly says, "And I'd go too."

The officer studies me. "Was anyone jealous of your friendship with Jack? They could've ransacked the place for personal reasons, because they had a vendetta."

My eyebrows shoot up. Whoever tossed the apartment might be making a point and getting back at Jack for some slight. There are many reasons to dislike Jack. He blurts out what he thinks without filtering first, and he mooches money. He borrows money but doesn't pay it back.

I say, "He can rub people the wrong way. I think my boyfriend is a bit jealous of Jack, who doesn't have a job while the rest of us work our tails off."

I close my mouth before I say too much in front of Kelly. When Buzz moved in with us, he asked me not to talk to Jack every day. Buzz wants to be the one I turn to with my problems. I agreed to back off but then old habits took over and I accepted Jack's calls, like I have for years.

I purse my lips and throw Craig under the bus. "Craig, the guy who was here this morning, made remarks about how Jack is a jerk, and someone needs to straighten him out."

The officer taps his pen on a notepad. "So, Craig has made what could be construed as threatening remarks?"

Kelly says to me, "Why didn't you tell me about this?"

"Because you didn't need to know. I thought Craig was just mouthing off. He's been upset with your dad about different things for years." To the officer, I say, "It's possible Craig tore up this place."

I chew on a fingernail. In the process of trying to find Jack and protect what he has, I'm doubting everyone. I've become a traitor to my friends.

The officer jots down notes. "Where is Jack? Is he away on a trip?"

I say, "He was swept overboard yesterday afternoon. He's missing, and the Coast Guard is searching for him."

Kelly wipes her eyes, and I pat her shoulder.

The officer snaps his notepad closed. "That's all for

now. We'll be in touch if we learn anything." As he walks out, he says, "I hope you aren't planning on staying here tonight. It'd be best if you stayed elsewhere, in case the intruder comes back."

I give Kelly a look. The person who slashed the pillows might hurt us. "We're going to my house."

Kelly says, "You and Buzz didn't sound so friendly last time you talked. Are you sure?"

I shrug. "We'll get over it. No big deal."

She rolls her eyes. "You say that, but look what happened with Dad. Divorce."

My face heats, and I say to the officer, "Thanks very much for coming over."

"Glad to help. Remember, don't stay long here. It'd be best if you leave."

"What do we do with the paper taped to the end table drawer?"

"Leave it where it is for now." He disappears down the hall.

I close and lock the door. But as I turn away, someone knocks.

"Who is it?" I say, putting my ear to the door. I need time to look for Jack's notebook and examine the paper under the end table. Then we'll leave. Plus, the pizza is coming.

"It's Craig. Let me in."

I say, "Come back tomorrow. This isn't a good time."

"I need to come in. If you don't open the door, I'll use my key and let myself in."

I frown, wishing Jack wasn't as generous with his extra keys, sprinkling them around town. "There is no way you're coming in. I'll call the cops if you don't leave."

"I have a right to be here. I've been paying Jack's rent for the last five months."

I say to Kelly, "What's he talking about?"

She raises her hands. "I don't know."

Craig says, "Come on, let me in. We need to talk."

"You have five minutes, that's it."

42

I turn the lock and swing open the door. The hinges squeak. Craig comes in and slumps in a seat, running a hand over his face. He groans. He has dark circles under his eyes, and he looks as worn out as I feel.

Kelly and I sit opposite him, staying as far from him as we can. I've got to get him to tell me what he was looking for this morning.

I say, "What are you doing here?"

"I'm looking for a password to an account, and I can't find it. Jack said if anything ever happened to him, he'd leave it in a secret place in the apartment."

"Why were you paying his rent?"

"We were working on a project and helping the elderly. He needed money to tide him over until we finished the work and got paid."

Hairs on the back of my neck stand on end. He is lying, according to what Buzz said. I don't feel safe. But I want to learn about the scam preying on the elderly, so I say, "Tell me about how you're helping the elderly. What's involved? Maybe Kelly and I could help too."

He taps the table with an index finger and leans in. "I'll be honest with you. I've been working on this a long time, I mean for years, and it is just now about to come to fruition. If I tell you details, it'll jeopardize it. You'll have to wait for more information."

"Are senior citizens and retired people giving you money? Every penny matters to them, and they don't have much to spare."

He narrows his eyes. "I wouldn't say that's the case. Affluent retirees have money to burn, and they're looking for investment opportunities."

I say, "What was your investment opportunity?"

He says in a low voice, "Don't say a word about this beyond these walls. I don't want someone to copy the idea and compete with us. We've put together a reverse mortgage program, but it isn't affiliated with a bank, and we're offering it to older people at a low cost. We make a profit, homeowners get cash, and when they die, we end up with the home. Everyone wins." He sits back and smiles.

His face is earnest, but his averted eyes suggest he is lying. The story doesn't match what Buzz said they were doing. Craig could have twisted the truth or told us lies.

I say, "Is it legal to offer a reverse mortgage like that?

Don't you need regulatory oversight and have rules to follow?"

He crosses his arms. "Of course, we follow rules. They're just not the ones that apply to banks and other lending institutions. Our company is outside the scope of those regulations."

I tap my foot. What a pack of lies. I bet they're doing this off the books. Buzz was right, and Craig and Jack are taking advantage of vulnerable, older people. I say, "You said you were looking for a password, but if that's true, why were you looking at Jack's bank statements?"

His ears turn red, and he scowls. Usually, he shows me the jolly, party animal friendly version of himself. Now that I'm peeling back layers of the truth, he looks like he's ready to lunge at me.

His jaw tenses. "Like I said, I was looking for a password. If you don't believe me, that's your fault."

"Is money missing? Is that why you were here and you cut the couch cushions?"

A vein throbs in his forehead. His left eye twitches. He fidgets with his fingers. He says, "No money is missing. I've got it under control."

I nod at how he didn't deny my accusation that he trashed the place. "Give me your key. Don't come here again."

Kelly says, "That's right."

His head jerks back. "Jack gave me permission. I'll come by anytime I want."

I say, "No you won't. Permission is revoked. I don't trust you, and I don't want you here when Jack comes back. Kelly lives here part-time."

He stands and laughs. "You think he's alive after all this time? I hate to break it to you, but there's no way Jack is breathing on this planet. No one survives that long."

Kelly bursts into tears.

I say, "That was cruel and heartless, saying that. Give me your key, or I'll call the cops and say you broke in. You'll walk out in handcuffs."

"Fine, don't get your panties in a knot." He slaps the key on the table. "I don't know why we were friends. I never liked you anyway. You had Jack and Buzz twisted around your little finger, doing whatever you wanted. Good riddance."

I open the door and say, "You were trying to get in with the guys and be one of them. Go live your scummy life without us. Get out of here and don't come back."

He slams the door on his way out, and I hold my weeping daughter. A timid knock on the door taps lightly three times. I release Kelly and go to the door. "Who is it?"

"Mr. Abernathy from across the hall. Is everything all right in there? I heard yelling and wanted to check and see if you and Kelly are okay."

I swing the door open wide. "We just lost a friend, but we're going to be fine. Come on in."

43

Mr. Abernathy blinks when he sees Kelly blowing her nose. He's known her since she was born. He says, "I'm sorry to hear about your father going missing. What a terrible situation. I'm sure they'll find him and bring him home in no time."

I sigh. Kelly doesn't need people reminding her that Jack is gone, although I'm sure it's ever-present in her mind. Craig was a beast for flinging fears in Kelly's face. We have to hold out hope that he's alive. How quickly friendship can turn into hate. We'll need forgiveness to get over this, but I don't want to. I'm finished with Craig.

The neighbor talks in a quiet voice to Kelly, and her rigid shoulders drop. We have a lot to get done and not much time to do it. We've got to look for Jack's notebook, read the note under the bedside end table drawer, and search the place.

I say, "Could I ask you a favor?"

He nods, and fiddles with his glasses. "Sure, you bet."

"If someone comes by and asks for a key, would you please tell them you don't have one anymore? We've had too many people coming and going through Jack's apartment since he disappeared, and I want to keep his things intact."

"Fine with me. That makes sense. There have been a lot of people coming and going. Like the young woman in the middle of the night." He rubs his stubbled chin. "What was her name? I forget."

My eyes grow wide. "What did she look like?"

"She was big and tall, wearing sunglasses and a scarf over her hair, but it might have been a wig."

"What time did she come in?"

"She woke me up around one in the morning? She was really pounding hard. She must be a very strong woman."

I turn to Kelly, who is looking composed, with her hair up in a high ponytail. "Did your dad mention a woman like that? Do you think it was his new girlfriend?"

Kelly stares at the floor. "No, and I would've remembered if he did. He likes Gigi's Café and took me there a lot. Karina always gave him two scones when he ordered one."

Mr. Abernathy says, "I know Karina at the café and this wasn't her. In fact, the woman here looked like she needed to shave after a long day. She was so big she could've played football."

I put my hands on my hips. I'm jealous of Karina, but she's not going out with Jack, so my envy is misdirected. No wonder Buzz is jealous. This is what it feels like.

I frown. I'm trying to weave a tapestry with loose threads, and I need solid facts. Questions flit through my mind like birds in flight. Could Jack have set up an escape plan to avoid creditors? It is possible but unlikely.

My phone dings, and I check my texts. The Coast Guard suspended their active search for Jack, according to Mike. I pocket my phone. I'll tell Kelly later.

"What was that?" she says.

I shrug. "What do you mean?"

"The text. It made you upset. What's going on?"

I say, "It's not good news, and I'd rather not say."

She stomps a foot. "I'm old enough. Tell me."

I say, "The Coast Guard called off the active search for your father."

She gasps and covers her mouth. Her face turns pale.

Mr. Abernathy is silent for a beat before heading to the door. "I'm sorry to hear that. Let me know if you need anything. I'm right across the hall."

I lock the door behind him and say, "Let's hold out hope that your dad is alive and getting warm somewhere. We can't give up hope. Not yet."

She nods and clenches her jaw, reminding me of her father. "What do we have to do before we get out of here?"

"See if we can find the notebook your dad wrote in. Look through his paperwork for anything related to reverse mortgages. See if Craig's name is on anything indicating they ran a business together. Look for something that mentions who he owes money to. Read whatever is written on the underside of the end table in the bedroom. And get the heck out of here."

She tilts her head. "Don't you need to make up with Buzz before we go home? You two didn't part on the best of terms from what I saw."

"You look for the notebook. I'll call Buzz. The pizza sure is taking a long time to be delivered, isn't it?"

44

———

When I call Buzz, he picks up right away. "What's going on?" he says. "Is everything okay?"

"She's upset they called off the search. Craig came by, but I kicked him out. And I don't like the way you and I left things."

"Me neither," he says. "I love you."

"Love you too. Let's talk after this blows over."

"I was thinking the same thing. We've got to make some changes."

I wince because he made it sound ominous. "We'll be here a while. See you later."

I hang up and bite my lip. I didn't want to get into it over the phone with Kelly listening. And the police officer told us to leave. We've got to get out of here.

She says, "Help me turn over the couch. He might have hidden it there."

I help her flip over the couch, and we examine the underside, finding no rips or tears in the fabric. We don't find Aretha Franklin's third handwritten will or Jack's notebook.

I say, "Keep looking. I'll go in the bathroom."

I push aside bath towels and rolls of toilet paper on the bathroom closet shelves. No notebook or secret stash of papers catch my eye. I shove it all back and march to living area and kitchen.

Kelly is rummaging around in cabinets with her back turned to me.

I say, "Find anything?"

"Not yet, just lots of dust."

I open the freezer, because on TV shows that is where people hide their secret stash of loot. There's an ice cube tray, a frozen pizza, and nothing else.

I rip open the cardboard pizza box, expecting to find passwords to a bank account or precious documents wrapped in a plastic bag. "Nothing here."

I toss the pizza, still in the plastic wrapper, back in the freezer but stop when I see a Post-it note taped to the bottom of the pizza that shows: BrunoSwaggo123#.

I wave it in the air and grin. "Found something."

Kelly comes over. "What is it?"

"This could be the password to a secret bank account."

"What do we do with it?"

I gesture to a drawer. "We put it in a plastic baggie and take it with us."

Just then, someone pounds on the apartment door. I flinch and look at Kelly. She grabs my arm. I'm glad we're not staying here tonight. "Who is it?"

"Pizza delivery from Mr. Maggio's Pizza."

"I didn't order a pizza from there," I say through the door. "I called another place. Go away."

"Someone ordered it for you. As a gift. Open up now, or it will get cold."

He is loud and his tone is menacing. I pull out my phone and text Buzz. "Come over to Jack's. A man is trying to get in, and we're here."

The delivery man says, "They ordered extra pepperoni and said it was how you like it."

My stomach growls. Kelly's does the same. She whispers, "I'm really hungry. Should we open the door?"

I say in a low voice, "Definitely not. We don't know who is out there. And he's from a fake pizza place. He probably just wants to get in and search the apartment."

He kicks the door, and we yelp and jump back.

"You'd better open the door if you know what's good for you. This pizza is getting colder by the minute."

I pull out my phone with shaking hands. "I'm calling the police."

"What's going on?" Mr. Abernathy says. "Why are you being so loud?"

He yelps and whimpers. Something hits the door in the hallway.

My pulse pounds in my ears, and I dial 911. When the dispatcher comes on the line, I report someone is trying to break in. I give Jack's address, and the dispatcher says a patrol car will arrive as soon as they can.

I lean against the door. "I called the police, and they're on their way. Mr. Abernathy, are you okay?"

All I hear is a grunt. Kelly makes to open the door, but I stop her. "We can't open it. Someone is out there, trying to get in."

"But it sounds like he's hurt."

I call through the door, "I called the police. You'd better leave."

The sounds of a pizza box dropping and heavy footsteps running down the hall come through the door.

Someone raps twice. "Let me in. It's Buzz. We need to help this older gentleman."

I open the door at the sound of his voice, fling my arms around his neck, and step back. "Let's get him inside and check his vital signs. The police are on the way."

Buzz, Kelly, and I lift Mr. Abernathy and place him on the couch cushions on the floor. I check Mr. Abernathy's wrist. "He's breathing, and he has a pulse."

He opens his eyes and groans. "Who was that guy? He punched me in the gut."

"We don't know," I say, "but he wanted to get inside the apartment."

Mr. Abernathy sinks back with a sigh. "He didn't have pizza in the box he was carrying. He pulled out a pistol."

Kelly and I look at each other with wide eyes, because the man could have shot us through the door. Or, he could have broken in and killed us. "You saved our lives," I say, squeezing his hand. "Rest until the police arrive. Do you want a glass of water?"

He blows out a breath. "Yes, please."

When Kelly brings him a glass of water, he sits up, arranges his gray comb-over hair, and sips. "Lots of excitement on a dull day," he says with a chuckle. His eyes are bright, and he's smiling. "I'll tell the guys at the senior center when we play pool tomorrow, but they won't believe me. A guy with a gun carrying a pizza box? It's too far-fetched to believe."

My gaze snags on Buzz, and we nod to each other. The situation has become dangerous. Jack was involved in a scam with life and death consequences. If he did intend to disappear, which I doubt, I understand why. People are determined to find out what my former husband was up to, and I won't loiter long here with my daughter. At any moment, someone might barge in, bust up the place, and hurt or kill us.

I swallow. We're not safe, and we must go. But I need to find a few quick answers before we leave. Jack's disappearance is the match that lit the fire, and his place is like a boat with a leaking fuel tank, about to burst into flames and take the rest of us with it.

45

─────────

I say to Kelly, "We've got to get out of here. But before we go, I want to finish looking for your dad's notebook."

She throws up her hands. "I've looked everywhere. I can't find it."

Mr. Abernathy says, "Your father gave me something to hide before he went boating yesterday. He said not to give it to anyone, no matter who asked, and he planned to come back for it one day."

I blink, because Jack gave a lot of thought to preparing before he was swept overboard. Was he on the bow that afternoon because he was planning to jump and make it look like an accident? Maybe I mucked up the works by hanging around him and yammering on about the need for a personal floatation device. No wonder he looked vexed with me. Standing here now, it seems more and more obvious that Jack set up a plan to disappear. It sounds wild and death-defying, because he could have died trying to escape that way. Who knows if he made it to the shoreline or to a waiting boat?

I pick at a cuticle as a stray thought flits past. Was Buzz part of Jack's escape plan? Where was Buzz when the rest of us were searching in our boats and coordinating by marine radio? He was absent during part of the search. What if he picked up Jack and took him to waiting car with fresh clothes?

I shake my head at the absurd notion. There's no way Jack and Buzz would do that. And Buzz wouldn't keep a secret from me. We're two open books with each other. We tell each other everything.

Kelly says to the neighbor, "Is it a notepad with his writing? About this big?"

She holds up her hands showing the measurements, and Mr. Abernathy nods. "That's right."

She puts her hands together and says in a pleading voice, "Would you please give it to me? It was important to my dad, and now he's missing. I'm sure he'd want me to have it. I'm his daughter, after all."

I nod. Go get 'em, Kelly. She's eloquent and deter-mined, and I'm bursting with pride as her mother.

Buzz says, "Maybe you'd better hand it over to me for safekeeping. I wouldn't want the girls to get hurt."

I cross my arms. "We're not girls. We're women with minds of our own."

Buzz holds up his hands. "Sorry I offended you. But I have a safe where I can keep it. That way no one will get hurt if someone is looking for it."

Just then, a police officer knocks on the open door. I cringe, realizing I should have closed and locked the door after the man fled. I wasn't thinking straight after the shock and assumed he wouldn't come back. We're lucky he didn't return with two buddies as back up.

A female officer says, "You called about an intruder?"

I gesture for her to come in. "Yes, I was the one who called."

She enters and looks around. "Is the person still on the premises?"

"No, they ran off."

"What did they look like?"

I turn to Mr. Abernathy. "You saw him."

He clears his throat. "He was big and built like a Mack truck, all muscle. He had a baseball cap pulled down over his eyes."

The officer whips out a small pad and takes notes. "Age?"

Mr. Abernathy shrugs. "Hard to say. Maybe thirty. I'm not a good judge of age anymore. He had tattoos around his wrists."

"Dark hair? Light?"

"Couldn't tell, it happened so fast. But maybe dark brown. He punched me in the stomach and knocked me to the floor."

She jots this down. "We may need to get in touch with you later. What's your name, address, and telephone number?"

He gives his name, address, and digits. "I live across the hall. I've been a neighbor for years."

The officer looks around. "You don't live here?"

"Nope."

"Who lives here then? Did the man with the gun ransack the place?"

I say, "He didn't come inside. My daughter and I were here with the door locked, and Mr. Abernathy stopped him. Whoever tossed the place was here today. I reported it to the police."

Kelly says, "My dad lives here, but he's missing. He was swept overboard in a boating accident yesterday. We're looking for him."

The officer says, "Seems like a lot of people are looking for more than your dad, from the state of this place."

I nod. Like a boat at sea with the wind blowing twenty-knots, we're lost in a storm of questions, and I have no idea how to work my way out. I grit my teeth. I'd better find a way forward, because Jack's fate is at stake and Kelly is depending on me.

Buzz says, "We don't know what they're after." He says to me, "Do you have any idea why people have searched the apartment?"

I shake my head. "I haven't a clue."

The officer eyes us, Kelly, Buzz, Mr. Abernathy, and me, brought together by Jack's disappearance. She takes down Jack's name and occupation, which Buzz gives as bartender. She says, "This is suspicious. The place is tossed after someone goes missing. And the man with the gun was trying to break in. Do I have the facts right?"

I say, "Yes."

Buzz says, "That's correct."

She says to Mr. Abernathy, "Did you get a good look at the gun?"

He shakes his head. "I'm not sure what type it was. It happened so fast. He pulled it out of a pizza box and pointed it at the door."

She says, "We'll take this seriously. It sounds like it could have been a home invasion, which is rare in our area, if you hadn't come along. I'll go back to the station and see what we can find. Did you get a look at the car he was driving?"

Mr. Abernathy, who is now my hero, says, "I did hear a loud car pull up to the curb out front, and I looked out. I saw the guy get out of a red car with a bad muffler, and he was carrying a pizza box."

"Did you get the license plate?" the officer says.

"No, I didn't, and I wish I had."

She stops at the threshold. "I advise you to vacate the premises as soon as possible and stay somewhere else tonight. Whoever it was may come back."

I glance at Buzz and say, "We're leaving soon. Thanks for coming by,"

"Yes, thank you," Buzz says, intertwining his fingers with mine.

We sound like oldsters saying goodbye to neighbors who stopped by for tea and cookies. This whole incident has me out of whack. I give Buzz a side glance. I have a hunch he might have had something to do with Jack's disappearance. But I have no proof, just intuition and feelings, for suspecting Buzz of being complicit. I'll have to trust him, or our new relationship will never get off the ground.

46

———

I close the door and say to Kelly and Buzz, "We have a lot to do." Turning to Mr. Abernathy, I say, "Would you please give us Jack's notebook? I'll take good care of it until he comes back."

He stands, rising to his full height of five-foot five. "Family trumps everything, so that's fine with me. I think Jack wouldn't mind it at all. After that hooligan socked the stuffing out of me, I'd like to get it off my hands." He frowns. "I hope it won't bring you trouble. Jack seemed to be mixed up in something this last month, with all kinds of characters knocking on his door at all hours of the day and night."

I turn to my daughter. "When you stayed here on your dad's nights, were people coming by at all hours?"

She says, "Yeah, but Dad told me not to mention it. He

didn't want you to get mad or say I couldn't come over as much."

I shake my head. "I'll get the notebook from Mr. Abernathy, then we'll get out before the man with the gun comes back."

I go across the hall to the neighbor's apartment. Unlike Jack's, which has a bachelor pad bare bones feel, the neighbor's place is warm and inviting. Patterned area rugs soften the sound of our footsteps as I follow him into his study. Standing lamps cast off warm light. Bookshelves remind me that Mr. Abernathy likes to read. A cushioned tan leather chair and ottoman look like a good place to sit with a book and look out the window.

He gives me a worn school notebook and says, "Here you are. It is your responsibility now."

I tuck it under my arm. "Thanks, I'll keep it safe. Do you have my cell number, in case you need help?" He nods. I say, "If that man with the pizza box comes back, call the police. And then give me a call to give me a heads up? I'd appreciate that."

"I will. I'll get my baseball bat and archery set out of the hall closet to defend myself if he tries to come in. I'll keep my cell phone with me and next time, if it happens, I won't go out in the hall and get involved."

I pat his shoulder. "Good, because I don't want anything to happen to you."

Back in Jack's apartment, my stomach churns with

anxiety. The pizza box guy might turn up at any minute. A vein in my temple pulses. Kelly and Buzz rush around searching the apartment for more clues to what Jack was doing.

My hands shake as I reach under the kitchen sink, which is overflowing with dirty plates and cereal bowls, and pull out a pair of yellow rubber gloves I insisted Jack have on hand for heavy-duty cleaning jobs. I snap them on and take a clean plastic baggie from a drawer.

"Mom, what're you doing? You're not washing dishes, are you? Leave them for later, like Dad does."

Buzz cocks his head. "We only have a few minutes at most to take a last look around and leave before the guy comes back."

I say, "I'll get that piece of paper from the underside of his bedside table."

I stride to Jack's bedroom and glance at the closed door to the room with his sneaker collection. My pulse picks up. I don't have time to stop and check the other bedroom. I hurry to Jack's bedroom.

Kelly calls, "But why the gloves?"

"To preserve fingerprints." I peel off the note, tuck it in the bag, and rip off the gloves, tossing them on the floor. The apartment is already a mess, leaving these won't make a difference. Besides, who knows if Jack will ever come back.

I grab Jack's gym bag out of the closet, stuff in the

plastic baggie with the note and add the notebook Mr. A. gave me. A Reader's Digest book on top of the dresser catches my eye. The dark blue cover shows a block of green with gold lettering. I've never seen it before. I shove it in the bag and bolt for the living room. "I've got everything. You guys ready?"

Buzz and Kelly are sitting on the floor gazing at a scrapbook with photos of our group of friends in high school. They look up and stare, as if locked in a time long ago.

I say, "Let's go."

My phone rings, and I glance at it to see who is calling. It is Mr. Abernathy from across the hall, so I answer.

He says in a rushed voice, "The red car came back. The man with the gun is climbing out right now."

"Call the police," I say. "We'll go out the back way. Thanks for the heads up."

My heart races. I sling my purse over my shoulder cross-wise, to be more agile if we have to run, and grab the gym bag.

Buzz and Kelly jump to their feet.

He says, "I'm taking the scrapbook. I don't want it ruined."

We rush out to the hall. and I lock the door with trembling hands.

The entry door on the floor below slams with a thud.

I point to the right and whisper, "Go."

Kelly nods. Her chin quivers. Buzz takes her arm and propels her down the hall.

My hands turn cold. What if we don't make it in time? What will we do, armed with a book and memories stored in an old scrapbook?

We run for the rear exit.

47

We hurry down the back stairway. The sound of someone pounding on a door reaches our ears. I cringe and hope Mr. Abernathy will be okay. We race down the steps.

Buzz says, "We'll get through this. We've made it through tough times before."

I flash him a smile as we burst outside, running to our cars.

He says, "We'll go in my car."

I grasp my daughter's hand. "I'll take my car. I don't want to leave it here."

He says, "We don't have time to argue about it. Let's go."

But my car is right there, a foot away. I can't leave it in the gravel parking lot. The four-door sedan is my only land transportation and represents my freedom and independence.

The wind picks up and whistles past. Trees sway, and leaves fly by. Wood cracks and splinters, and a big tree branch falls down, smashing the hood of a nearby car.

Catalyzed by the growing storm and impending danger, I say, "We'll take separate cars. See you there. Come on, Kelly. Get in my car." I unlock the doors and toss Jack's gym bag and my purse on the back seat. Energy thrums through me. In a matter of minutes, the thug might come out and chase us down.

She stands frozen between us. We're exposed in the parking lot and could be seen through the upstairs windows. Jack's apartment faces the other way, but I'm not taking chances. "Let's go."

She stands with her hand on Buzz's car door. "Meet you there," she says.

I hop in my car, crank up the engine, and drive away. My daughter has shown her first inkling of having an independent streak and veering away from her mother's influence. I don't think I'm ready for more of this.

Buzz and Kelly follow me. Wind buffets my car. Sprinkles of rain dot the windshield, and I turn on the wipers. Glancing in the rear-view mirror, I see the red car a few car lengths behind Buzz. I clench my jaw and make a decision. I'll protect my daughter and let them get ahead by calling attention to myself.

I pull over, wave Buzz ahead, and point down the road.

He drives by with his eyebrows raised in a question, and I say, "Go, go."

My heart thuds. Blood whooshes in my ears. My hands are moist as I pound on the accelerator, turn the wheel, and screech to a halt at an angle, blocking both lanes. I grab a t-shirt from the back seat, wrap it around my head like a scarf, and shove sunglasses on. I hop out and pop the hood, pretending to look inside to see what's wrong.

The fake pizza delivery guy brakes hard and his tires screech as he comes to a sudden stop. My pulse quickens. I hope my distraction will give Buzz time to get away with Kelly. I might have made the biggest mistake of my life, and Kelly could end up without both parents, but I'll do what I must to keep my daughter safe.

The man honks his horn. His broad face is flushed. He may have anger management issues, but it's not my business. He shakes a fist and yells, "Get out of the way!"

I open my hands and do my best to look like I can't move my car from blocking the two-lane road.

He heaves his large body out of the car and lumbers over. He's over six-feet-tall with broad shoulders and packing three hundred pounds or more. Veins stand out on his temples. His hands are the size of small dinner plates.

I peer under the hood of my car. I can't get the better of him physically, so I'll use my mind, and it's easy to appear fascinated by mechanics, given my penchant for repairing engines. Heavy footsteps approach. Rain drums on the car hood above my head, and I fiddle with the fan belt.

He says in a gravelly voice, "Get this wreck off the road. I'm in a hurry, and you're blocking my way."

I frown. "I wish I could, but the car quit. The darn thing stopped all of a sudden."

My feet sweat in my socks. I'm quaking in my sneakers, but I've got to remain calm. Kelly and Buzz need time to get somewhere safe.

He curses. "Come on, I don't need this with the boss breathing down my neck. I'm working right now, lady, and you're holding me up."

I suppress a grimace, thinking of how he hit Jack's neighbor. I'm a little bit offended at being called a lady, but I let it go under the circumstances. I put on a Minnesota accent, where my mother came from. "You betcha, and I'm very sorry, but I can't get the car going. It conked out. And who might your boss be? I'll put in a good word for you. Would you like me to speak with them?"

He scowls. "Forget it, it's none of your business. Hey, don't I know you from somewhere? Weren't you back in that building?"

"Me, no, I was just coming home from the store. Had to buy more cat food for the seventeen cats I have. Even feral ones need a home, you know?"

He frowns. "This sure is a nosy town. Everyone is in

each other's business, and I'm sick of it. I need everyone to butt out, so I can get the job done."

I tilt my head and fold my arms. "What job is that? I'm curious. Inquiring minds want to know."

He bounces on his toes and clenches his fists. "Like I said, butt out. It's nobody's business but mine."

I play a hunch. "Are you working for Bill Rafferty? Did he send you?"

His eyes grow wide, and his fists unfurl. "What? No. Why'd you ask about him? He's a two-bit pawn broker and nowhere near in the league of my boss. She runs a huge operation." He spits on the two-lane blacktop.

I tap a toe and keep him talking. "So, you work for a woman. What's her name?"

He snarls, shakes a fist, and strides to his car. "When I'm through with what I came here for, I'm leaving this place and never coming back. There are way too many busybodies in Millersville. You need to get lives of your own. Find a hobby, like crossword puzzles, instead of pestering strangers. That's what I do."

He hops in his car, slams the door, and revs up the engine. The car surges ahead, and I leap out of the way just in time. His car slams into my left front fender. Metal crunches, and the sound makes my hands clench. I swallow and worry he'll track down Buzz and Kelly or come back and hurt me. My armpits prickle with sweat. Tires squeal as he accelerates down the road and rounds the corner.

I blow out a shaky breath. At least I delayed him a few minutes. I hope Buzz had enough time to get out of sight and hide Kelly.

Rain lashes my face, and tears run down my cheeks. All I want is to be safe with my daughter, tucked away in our house with Buzz cooking dinner and a fire blazing in the fireplace.

Jack being washed overboard has rocked us all. I'm suspicious and suspect my friends of nefarious wrong doings. My friends and I trusted each other and knew each other's secrets. But I knew nothing.

A gust of wind slams into me, making my hair fly across my face. Cars form a line in both directions. I'm blocking the road, and I'm thoroughly knotted up and confused. I need help. I can't do this alone.

48

Cars are backed up in both directions. A woman taps on the horn, and her electric vehicle issues a diminutive bleat. That riles up the others, and cars of all sizes and shapes honk. A man in his sixties wearing a plaid flannel shirt hauls himself out of a crew cab pickup. "Do you need help?"

"No, but thanks very much." I jump in my car and drive away, heading toward home. But a few blocks later, a thought occurs to me. Violet is an expert at protecting clients and ferreting out information, and I could use her help. I pull off to the side of the road, park on a corner, and pull out the business card she gave me at Gigi's Café.

The fake pizza delivery guy drives past on a side road. He's hunched over the wheel and shouting into a cell phone. I duck down to stay out of sight.

When I dial Violet's cell, she picks up on the first ring.

"Outrigger Services. This is Violet. How can I help you?"

"Violet, this is Irena Fishbone. I need your help. Do you have time to meet?"

"Sure, what day and time work for you? Sometime next week?"

Thunder rumbles. My wipers squeal across the windshield. I clear my throat. "Things are a mess. I was hoping we could meet right away. Is that too much to ask?"

"Hold on, I'll check with my team." She muffles the phone, calls out to someone, and comes back on the line. "Sure, come over right away if you can. I'll meet with you and get Vincent and Mimi in on it too. Do you know where our offices are?"

I glance at the card. "I'll be there in five or ten minutes if I can grab a parking spot close by. I might have to park at the marina and run over."

She chuckles. "Don't get washed away. It's coming down hard out there."

"Thanks so much, See you soon."

Before I take off, I call Buzz. "How are you guys? Is everything all right?"

"Yeah," he says, "we're okay. I got us back to your place and closed the curtains. I thawed chili from the freezer for dinner. What happened with you?"

The tremor in his voice tells me he's concerned about me. I say, "How's Kelly?"

I hear his warm smile over the phone line. "She's doing great. She's worried about you though. Here she is."

"Mom, you shouldn't have taken off like that. Something could've happened to you."

"I wanted you to be safe."

"It goes both ways. I only have one parent right now, and I need to make sure you're safe."

"Thanks, sweetie. I love you too. Listen, I need you to hang out there for a while. I'm going to meet with someone who might be able to figure out why people are breaking into your dad's and find him."

"I want to go with you."

"This meeting won't take long and they're waiting for me, so I'll drive over and tell them what I know. I have no idea if they'll find anything meaningful. It may be a waste of time."

She sighs, and I realize she's stuck in the middle of the mess Jack left, and she's lost her father. I say, "Tell you what. I'll pick you up, and we'll go together. How's that?"

"Really?"

"Really. I'll see you soon. Put Buzz on the line, will you?"

I start the car and drive. Buzz comes on the phone and says, "What's going on? I was hoping you'd come back here, and we'd have time to talk."

"Remember how Violet, Karina's half-sister, offered to help? I'm going to meet with her, and I'm taking Kelly with me. When I come back, we need to sit down and talk, just the two of us. I have a lot of questions about you and Jack."

He clears his throat. "I want to be there when you speak with Violet. Jack is my friend, and I can add a new perspective."

I suppress a groan. Like everything after Jack disappeared, plans are getting complicated. I can deal with boat disasters and fix an engine, but I can't figure this out. I like things tidy, which this isn't. I like being in control and taking charge, which I know, isn't the most conducive to being in a loving relationship.

I turn the corner and drive to my house. "It'd be great to have you there. It's not just me who lost a friend. You must feel the loss and grief, although we haven't had time to talk about it. I'm coming down the street and will be there in about two minutes. See you soon, love you."

"Love you too," he says and hangs up.

49

I drive down my tree lined street past bungalows and tap the steering wheel, eager to pick Buzz and Kelly up and head to Violet's office. The secrets I've learned since Jack went missing have me questioning everything. Details swirl around in my mind. I hope Violet and her team will help solve the puzzle, because I can't do it on my own. I want Kelly to know what happened to her dad, otherwise questions will pester her for the rest of her life. We need to know if Jack was running a scam, if he meant to leave us, and if he planned his disappearance. I doubt he'd do that, but maybe I didn't know him at all.

Kelly and Buzz are waiting outside at the curb. I drive up, and they hop in, with Buzz taking the back seat and Kelly riding shotgun.

I say, "I hope Violet can help us."

Kelly nods. "Craig called me and said Dad stole the money and ran off with it."

I continue on, gripping the steering wheel tight. Only a jerk would call my daughter and upset her like that. "Craig called?"

Buzz leans forward. "Yeah, he did, and Kelly, if he calls you again, hang up or give the phone to me. He shouldn't be calling and talking about your dad."

A car honks as I roll through an intersection without stopping. I didn't see the stop sign. I cringe and keep going, vowing to pay better attention. "I agree. It's like he had a personality bypass, and we lost the nice guy we knew. Maybe this is who he always was, but he was covering it up."

Buzz says, "He was a great guy to hang out with, but he always had a hard edge."

Thinking back to the incident in the empty ballroom at Fir Island during high school, when he grabbed my neck in the dark and scared me so much, I say, "He did."

His eyes meet mine in the rear-view mirror, and he says, "We won't be hanging out with him again. We've come to the end of an era. Our group imploded when Jack went overboard."

Rain drops smack the windshield, and the wipers work hard to keep up. I pull into a parking space and say, "The history is there, but the trust is gone."

We hop out into the wind and rain. I pull up my sweat-shirt hood, sling an arm around Kelly's shoulder and say,

"I'm sorry you're going through this. We'll get through it, like we always have."

We hurry to Outrigger Services, and she says, "I don't care what Dad did. I just want him to come back."

I say, "I want him back too."

Behind us, Buzz coughs, like something is stuck in his throat.

"I hope Violet will figure out what's going on," I say, "and find your dad."

Buzz coughs again.

I turn to him. "Are you okay?"

He swallows. "Just fine."

Deep within, doubts form at the back of my mind. I have a feeling something precious at the base of our mountain has shifted in a relationship earthquake, and we won't return to how we were. Without being here, Jack has upended our lives.

We enter a two-story building and leave the wind and rain, hurrying up the stairs to Outrigger Services. Kelly isn't out of breath because she dances. Buzz is fit and takes long strides, while I lumber up the stairs with labored breaths in one more reminder that I've got to get in shape.

I say to Buzz, "This is a crazy time, isn't it?"

"It sure is," he says.

Kelly gets there first and holds the door open for us. As I pass through, she says, "I have a feeling Dad's alive. He's out there somewhere. We just need to find him."

I blow out a breath of sorrow for my sweet daughter

and regret that she is forced to go through this. She's too young to be hit by a devastating loss. Although I know there is never a good age for a gut-wrenching event to demolish lives and whip up calm seas into choppy turmoil, like when my father was sent to prison when I was young. I say, "I hope so. We're trying our best to get him back."

We walk in to an open reception area with three chairs. Beyond is a larger room with four chairs at work stations. Violet greets us with open arms. "Welcome, I see you brought reinforcements. Let me introduce you to my team. We'll do our best to help you."

Kelly bites her lower lip and looks on the verge of tears. Buzz stands with his feet apart. He takes my hand and holds it with a firm grip. My hands shake. I'm afraid of what we might find out. We're ignorant and on the edge of a cliff, about to jump off into the sea of knowledge. Or so I hope.

I say, "Thanks for meeting us on short notice. You know Buzz, and this is my daughter, Kelly."

Violet nods. "We met before at Gigi's Café." She walks up to Kelly, takes her hand, and looks into her eyes. "We're going to do everything we can to bring your dad home. We're experts in figuring things out and finding people, isn't that right, guys?"

She turns to a muscled man with chiseled cheekbones and a woman in her early thirties with dark curly hair. They nod and stand with their hands in a fig leaf pattern in front of them. They both say, "That's right, boss."

Violet says, "This is Vincent and Mimi, and they'll sit in on the meeting."

A younger woman stands from a desk in back. "And I'm Flora."

Violet says, "Sorry, Flora, I didn't mean to leave you out. Let's sit in the bullpen, and you can tell us what brought you here. It sounds bigger than a missing person's case, is that right?"

I take a plastic folding chair, and Buzz sits by me, with Kelly on my other side. I say, "We think so. Jack Fishbone fell overboard, and he's missing, but we've learned a lot since then. He might've been into some questionable activities, maybe even running a scam."

Buzz frowns. "He told me he was, but I don't have proof."

Kelly says, "My mom and dad were swept overboard by a rogue wave. He wasn't wearing a life jacket, and we've been looking for him." She looks at me.

I push on a cuticle and wish Kelly wasn't here. Learning the details might make her more worried. But she's a smart kid and probably knows as much as I do. I say, "The Coast Guard called off their active search and rescue operation. And the police said it's too soon to declare him a missing person."

I continue, "The wave took him by surprise, just like me. But we're hearing he may have planned this, maybe to escape debts he owed. He was last seen wearing a shirt, shorts, and flip flops. The Coast Guard found part of one of his flip flops we think. And I found his shirt nailed to a log floating near Cedar Island with writing in the collar."

Violet and her team glance at each other and scribble notes. Violet says, "What exactly did the writing say?"

I say, "The writing inside the collar in black felt tip marker said let me go and don't look for me, or something like that, which doesn't make sense."

Buzz chimes in. "There have been break ins at his apartment, which is super odd. That's never happened before. A man showed up earlier today pretending to deliver pizza. He was pounding on the door and about to break in. When the neighbor came out, he pulled a gun on him. The poor neighbor was punched in the stomach."

I hold up an index finger. "And, when I stopped by Jack's place before dawn, our friend Craig was there looking through financial papers."

The team jots this down.

Violet says, "Anything else?"

I say, "The apartment was vandalized today, like someone was looking for something. Cushions were ripped. Papers thrown all over."

Kelly puts her hands on her hips. "They stuck my hairbrush down the toilet." She wrinkles her nose.

"That's disgusting," I say. I didn't know that. I wonder what else she hasn't told me, but we haven't had time to sit and share. The same is true of Buzz and me. We really need a quiet hour to hang out, drink wine, and talk about what's going on. But I have a feeling the opportunity won't present itself soon, with chaos rearing its head.

Vincent's jaw tenses. He trains his eyes on me, and I squirm. I'd hate to be under his glare if I was a thief caught in the night. He says, "What was Jack up to that would cause this level of unwelcome attention? Anything on the shady side?"

I draw a deep breath. I'd like Kelly to have a positive image of her father. When Jack and I divorced, I vowed to myself not to say anything negative about him in front of her. But we've got to disclose the truth to these investigators. They have the skills to run down rumors, dispel lies, and uncover evidence of Jack's wrong doings, which might lead to finding him.

I say, "I heard Jack cooked up a reverse mortgage scam. Or, he was selling fake stock certificates in bankrupt companies over the phone."

Kelly chews on a fingernail. Buzz shifts in his seat. Violet nods. "Anything else?"

"There were large deposits," I say, "and withdrawals from his bank account, at least by my standards. I saw a few instances of ten-thousand-dollars moved in and out of his account last month."

Violet says to Buzz, "What about you? Anything you can add?"

He shrugs. "Our friend Craig said Jack was the ringleader, but I'm not sure about that. Craig always had some sort of scheme going to get rich, but most of the time, his grand plans would flop."

Violet looks up from her iPad. "We'll need Jack's full legal name, birth date, social security number and last known address. And the names of anyone else involved, like Craig. And what about the pizza delivery guy with a gun? We need a full description for him."

Kelly's face turns pale.

I say, "He's about six-feet tall, built like a football player, and has tattoos on his wrists. He drives a red sedan. I think he's still in town."

Mimi cocks her head. "How do you know that?"

"I saw him driving when I was going home, before we came here. He rammed my left front bumper, so his car will be scraped or have a crumpled right front of his car, maybe a broken headlight."

I stretch my tight shoulders. I want to take a walk and clear my head. I glance out at rain pelting the windows.

Violet stands. "Mimi will take the details from you about Jack." She points at the three of us. "I don't want you going near Jack's place until we clear this up. It's too dangerous. We don't know who might barge in if you're there. You could get hurt."

Kelly's chin quivers. "But I left my leotard there. I need it for dance class."

"I'll buy you another one," I say. "We can't take the risk."

She says, "But I liked that one."

I frown and blame Jack for my problems. A flock of regrets fly through my mind. We wouldn't be meeting and trying to solve the mystery he left behind if he wore a life jacket. If he wasn't addicted to buying sneakers, he would have paid me child support. If he wasn't a fool, we would have attended Kelly's dance recital, and the last two days would turned out entirely different.

Buzz takes my hand in his. "Everything okay? You look lost in thought."

I look at him and wonder if he is hiding secrets, like Jack was. But I say, "It's all good." A little lie doesn't hurt, if it makes him feel better.

I give Jack's birth date and other information to Mimi, and turn to go. Walking to the door, it dawns on me that I have a double standard. It is fine for me to fib, but I don't tolerate it in others. When I have time, I'll mull that over. It might not be the best way to operate.

50

We leave Outrigger Services and tromp down the steps in silence, each lost in our thoughts. I'm convinced Jack didn't plan this. You don't arrange for a rogue wave if you want to disappear and start a new life. Besides, we're not even sure he can swim.

We climb in the car, and Kelly turns to me with a worried look. "Why didn't you tell Violet what you found in Dad's frig? We should've told them everything."

I glance in the rearview mirror to check Buzz's reaction. The piece of paper Jack hid in the plastic potato is in my pants pocket, and I haven't had a chance to tell Buzz what I found. I was keeping it a secret until I knew what to do with the numbers. I can't let it get into the wrong hands.

He sits forward in the back seat. "What're you talking about?"

"Jack hid some information in his refrigerator, and they might be numbers for a bank account. I wanted to be sure, before I told anyone."

"Anyone?" he says with a scowl. He raises his voice. "I'm not just anyone. For crying out loud, we're living together."

I drive the last block to our house with the image of our love dashed on the rocks flashing before me. We could design a navigation chart for love. The word danger would appear above a hidden underwater hazard at the four-month mark, which is where we are. He moves in would have a flashing yellow warning sign for caution. Buzz joined the Kelly and me show, and it can't be easy on him.

I say, "There's a lot I haven't told you yet. We need to talk. And I have a feeling there are a few things you haven't told me too."

He sits back and stares out the window. "Maybe."

A thought flits through my mind. What is he hiding? But I push it away. I'm sure he wouldn't hold anything back. We've known each other forever.

As I pull into the driveway, Kelly says, "We need to look at that note too."

We get out of the car, and Buzz says, "What note?" He holds out his hands. "No more secrets between us, okay?"

I smile. "Great, we'll be straight with each other from now on."

The dog greets us, barking. We let him out, and he does his business and races inside out of the rain, shaking and getting us wet in the process. Buzz strides to the kitchen and pulls out two bottles of beer, handing me one. "I thought we were straight with each other. You're making me uneasy." He perches on the couch.

Kelly comes in with a glass of water and flops on an easy chair. She says, "Let's take a few minutes and then look for clues?"

Buzz and I nod and give each other a half-smile at how grown up she is.

She says, "I liked how Violet and her team approached the problem. It's interesting what they do. I might want to do that one day."

My eyebrows shoot up. "I'm not sure I want you doing that, if there's an element of danger."

She flings her legs over the arms of the chair. "I'm not a kid anymore, and we're past the time when you make my life decisions for me. It's my life, not yours to live."

I wince. "You're right, and what you do for work will be your choice. I'm just not used to you being so grown up."

She says, "I'll make mistakes and learn from them. I've watched Dad, and I don't want to be like him, stuck in jobs he hates, and maybe desperate enough to scam innocent old people. If he was doing that."

I let out a breath. She's as strong-headed as I am, so I

had better back off, or I'll end up pushing her away. "We're not sure if he was involved in illegal scams. Maybe Violet can find out."

Buzz rests his elbows on his knees. "I heard him on the phone a few times, before he realized I was listening. I'm pretty sure he was wrapped up in stuff he could be arrested for. He wouldn't talk about it, even though I tried to get him to confide in me. I told him to get out of whatever it was before it was too late."

Tears stream down Kelly's cheeks, as if every word about Jack wounds her.

I say, "There's a chance he might still be alive."

The dog nudges her leg, and Kelly says in a tight voice, "How big a chance is it?"

I raise an eyebrow at Buzz and wish he hadn't broken my daughter's heart by bringing up the subject of Jack's fate. She doesn't need to be reminded that he may be fish food or a bloated body washed up on a beach.

"It's a slim chance, to be honest," I say. "But we can't rule out that he may be alive. Someone could be sheltering him in a shack. Maybe he can't get to a phone. He loves you, and if he's alive, he'll make his way back to you."

Buzz sits back, his leg leaning against mine. "Whatever it takes, he'll come back to you. He said you're his shining light and his brightest star."

Kelly breaks into a slight smile. "He did?"

He smiles and rubs the ears of his dog. "He did. He

told me his world revolved around you, and you're the most important person to him. He said his heart opened on the day you were born." He winks at me.

I chime in. "He loved you, and if it's possible, he'll come back for you."

She sniffs and says, "He can swim, can't he?"

I sigh. "He said he took swimming lessons a while back."

She says, "But he didn't always tell the truth, did he?"

I get up from the couch and give her a hug. "Not always. But let's hope he can swim, because it would help him survive and get to shore. Who knows, maybe he was the man who was jogging naked."

She tilts her head. "If it was Dad, he would've asked the painter woman for help. He wouldn't have run off."

Buzz shifts in his seat. "Maybe when we look back on this, we'll have all the answers, but right now, I'm stumped."

I say, "Nothing makes sense. I hope we'll learn something soon from Violet."

Kelly says, "You should've told them everything."

I nod. "When I see them again, I will."

Buzz says, "Tell me everything."

But before I can, my phone dings, and I pick it up. Bets texted to say, "We found something. Call me as soon as possible."

51

———————

I look up from my phone and tell Kelly and Buzz about the text from Bets. Kelly stands and says, "Call her now and put it on speaker, so we can hear what she says."

Buzz says, "Let's go in the kitchen. I'll make sandwiches while we talk with them." The dog follows him, tail wagging.

My stomach growls. "Good, I'm hungry."

In the kitchen, Kelly fills water glasses and puts them on the table. Buzz makes peanut butter sandwiches with sourdough bread. I slide into a seat at the table, and my hands tremble as I call Bets. I'm nervous about what we might hear. My pulse picks up when she answers the phone.

She says, "Glad you called. You won't believe what we found."

My hands are moist and I put the phone on the table, punching the button for speaker phone. I wipe my palms on my jeans. "Tell us."

In the background, her husband Zerk says, "Don't tell them right away. Build the suspense first. Explain how we went about it. We could be detectives instead of bartenders." He chuckles.

"This is my call," she says, "and I'll do it my way. You sit and listen."

"All right, sweet cheeks." A chair creaks in the background.

"Okay, where was I?" she says. "My darn husband distracted me with a capital d."

"What did you find?" Kelly blurts out.

"Right. We did some digging and drove around, monitoring certain people's activities when we weren't working at the Brown. Or the Lantern, as Zerk calls it."

Zerk says, "It's The Lantern, honey plum."

She says, "The Brown is what locals call it."

I roll my eyes at the bickering between two love birds. "Can we move on and jump to the part where you tell us what you found?"

Bets says, "Sure, so there we were, parked in a dark alley by Jack's place."

Zerk says, "Who do we see but your friend Craig coming out in the wee hours of the morning carrying a box. It looked light, like it was filled with papers, and had a lid on top. He dropped it in his trunk, looked around, and drove off."

My mouth falls open. "I told Craig not to go in Jack's apartment. He knew he wasn't supposed to be there. And what was he doing? Carrying out some of Jack's stuff?" I say to Kelly and Buzz, "We should report him to the police."

"We don't have proof," Kelly says, holding up her hands.

"I videotaped it," Bets says. "I'll send it to you. You can watch it with a bowl of popcorn, like a movie." Bets and Zerk chuckle.

"I doubt I'll have an appetite," I say, "watching a friend betray Jack."

Kelly says, "I live there some of the time. What if he took my stuff?"

Drumming my fingers on the table, details swirl in my mind. I am exhausted and hungry. I can't wait until this is over, and we figure out what's going on. The many possible explanations boggle my mind.

I tell her, "I bet Craig was after your dad's paperwork. When we can go back in, we'll see what's missing." A thought occurs to me, and I say, "Did your dad buy anything new or expensive in the last few weeks?"

Kelly says, "Yeah, he bought a violin."

I cock my head. "A violin?"

She shrugs. "He said he wanted to learn to play. But he wouldn't let me open the case or hold it."

I purse my lips. "This story is getting stranger and stranger. Jack never wanted to play an instrument before." I turn to Buzz. "Did he mention this to you?"

He shakes his head. "He never mentioned it. Not even the last time we hung out and had a heart-to-heart talk over beers at the Brown."

Bets says, "See, what did I say, hon. Locals call it the Brown."

Zerk says, "We need to take this friend of yours Craig seriously. He's sneaking around, not caring about the consequences. Tread carefully with him. He may be dangerous. We know that from experience, don't we sweet heart?"

They chuckle, sharing an inside joke. Not for the first time, I wonder what they did in their former lives when they lived in Nevada. They've been quite vague about the subject.

Bets says, "We've got to go now. You take care. We'll keep a look out for possible criminal activity." They laugh, and she hangs up.

52

M

y muscles ache. I get up from the chair and groan, stretching. I'm worn to a thin thread of worry about the whereabouts of my ex-husband. If I see him again, I'll tell him off for bringing a tornado of terror down on us, making us run around frantically searching for him.

"A violin?" I say to Kelly.

She and Buzz set plates with sandwiches on the table. All I want to do is sleep, but I've got to eat. My stomach growls. If only I could snap my fingers and have the answers. I pull out my phone and resist the urge to check with Violet. It is too soon, and they need time to piece together the puzzle. She doesn't need me getting in the way.

Kelly says, "Let's eat and then try to figure out what Dad was up to."

We chomp down and swallow, focused on the food. When my sandwich is gone, I finish drinking the water and set the glass down. I say to Buzz, "Are you sure you didn't know about the violin?"

He wipes his mouth with the back of his hand. "Nope, I didn't hear about that."

"It'd be a good place to hide papers. Maybe he didn't have a violin in the case."

Kelly says, "But I saw it. He showed it to me, but he wouldn't let me hold it."

I frown. "Then where is it?"

The doorbell rings, and we look at each other.

I say, "Are you expecting someone?"

Buzz stands and jams his hands in his pockets. "No, but I'll see who it is."

He glances out through the peephole in the door and turns to us with a shrug.

"Delivery," a man says. Rain spills over the gutter above the living room window.

The dog barks. Kelly says, "Open the door. Let's see what it is." She looks like she's expecting good news, but I suspect we'll be disappointed.

Buzz opens the door to a guy in his twenties with a man bun on top of his head. He's wearing black pants, a black t-shirt with no logo or emblem, and a blue rain jacket. I try to see his truck, but it's not in my line of sight.

Wind blows in through the open door. The dog tries to run past Buzz to get outside, but Buzz blocks him with his knee and grabs his collar. It's a three-ring circus, but chaos has been my middle name since Jack was swept into the Salish Sea.

The man hands Buzz a package the size and shape of a shoe box. "Sign here."

Buzz scribbles his signature, and the guy hurries to the street. He hops in the front passenger seat of a white van, and it drives off before I get a good look at the license plate.

Buzz shuts and locks the door. He leans against it and says, "Let's open this in the back yard, in case there's something inside that might explode."

I cringe and whisper to him as we head to the back door, "You're either brilliant or daft or both."

He smiles at me and says, "I'm all of those and ready to assist you where I can."

I throw my arms around him and kiss him.

Kelly says, "Get a room."

Buzz stops in the kitchen and gently places the box on the table. "You know what, it's nasty outside. We'll take a chance and open it here. I'm going crazy imagining all kinds of scenarios, and I bet it is just a pair of shoes meant for Jack."

I say, "But I don't understand why they'd be sent here."

"I agree," Kelly says. "But let's open it."

We gingerly pull off brown paper, and I set it aside in case we'll need it for forensic evidence. I chuckle to myself. I'm getting carried away with wild thoughts. The situation is straightforward. Jack fell in the water, he died, and nothing suspect is happening. The people who tossed his apartment got the wrong address. Everything is fine.

"The shoe box," Kelly says, "is taped shut."

She hands Buzz a pair of scissors, and he carefully cuts the tape. I lift the lid. A shiny gold card sits on top of white tissue paper. Kelly opens the card and reads aloud.

"Buzz, keep these for me until I get back. Hide them and don't let anyone see them. They are valuable, more than you'll ever know. By the time you read this, I'll be on my way to where the sun shines all year long. Don't worry about me. I'll be fine. By the way, give my love to Kelly and Irena. Jack."

Kelly scowls and is about to rip up the card when I grab it from her and tuck it in my pocket. She says, "Give my love to Kelly? Am I an afterthought? It sounds like he left on purpose. Why would he do that if he loved me?"

I say, "We don't have all the facts. This might have been sent as a distraction, or maybe we're reading more into it than we should. If he did move away, I'm sure he'd want to take you with him."

She sobs, and I hold her, patting her back like when she was a baby. She steps away and wipes her eyes. "I'm angry. Who would do this to their daughter?"

I nod. "I'm ticked off too." I turn to Buzz, "What do you think is going on?"

"I have no idea, but I want to see what's inside the box."

He pulls back the tissue paper and stares. Kelly and I hold hands. Before us is the most beautiful pair of shoes I've ever seen. The luscious gold leather has a red star sewed on the side of each shoe.

Buzz holds one up. "Must be a size thirteen or fourteen, triple-E wide. My cousin had wide feet. He would've died for a pair of shoes like this." He looks at us and shrugs. "But he passed away a while back."

Death is a frequent topic in our household lately. Thanks for bringing that up, Buzz, my love. I run a finger along the leather. The stitching is smooth. "Do you think it's a basketball shoe? It looks pretty fancy to wear playing sports."

Kelly says, "Dad's feet aren't this size. He's a size ten. He must've bought them for his collection or as an investment."

I laugh. "A sneaker as an investment? He's never sold any of his shoes, as far as I know." I smack my forehead. "I wish we'd checked his shrine to shoes in his second bedroom. Did either of you look in there? Maybe thieves wanted his shoes. Maybe Craig was carrying some out in a box."

Kelly says, "I opened the door real fast. It looked the same as always. Dad didn't like me going in there. Old habits, I guess."

I tap my chin. "But the shoes could've been rearranged, and the most valuable ones taken. Kelly, have you seen these gold leather shoes before? Maybe he knew something bad might happen, because he owed people money, and he hid these by sending them here."

She presses her lips together. "I've never seen them. And I would've noticed if they were in the room. Those are my favorite colors, red and gold. I'd like a pair of those shoes in my size."

I chew on a fingernail, pondering what to do next.

Buzz says, "I've never seen them before, and your dad took me in the room all the time, before our last argument, to show them off. He liked to brag and tell me about each shoe he owned. Where it was made, how much it cost, how much he estimated it was worth, like he was justifying his spending on shoes." He glances at me. "I wasn't a fan and told him it wasn't money well spent. He hated that."

I rest my hands on my hips. "I wish he'd used the money to pay for child support. Seeing this rubs it in my face, how irresponsible he was. It makes me so mad."

Kelly's mouth falls open. "He wasn't paying child support?"

"No."

"For how long?"

"Ten years."

"The whole time you've been divorced? You should've told me. I would've talked to him and made him pay. I would've dropped out of dance lessons."

I shake my head. "I didn't want you to suffer because

of his choices. That's why I work so hard. I pay for everything."

Buzz squeezes my hand. "Until I moved in. Now we'll split the costs."

I smile at him. What a relief it will be not to shoulder the financial burdens alone. I say, "I didn't want you thinking your dad was a dead beat, and I wanted you to stay a child for as long as possible. Besides, it was between us adults. I didn't want to involve you."

She crosses her arms. "Next time, don't keep secrets from me."

"I won't."

Buzz claps us on the back. "Don't you feel better, getting this out in the open?"

Kelly says, "Not really. I guess Mom was right not to tell me. What a selfish guy dad is. Or was." A tear trickles down her cheek.

"Hey, now," Buzz says, wiping away the tear. "We might find him, despite what the note says. He might be holed up in a fishing shack. You never know. Let's not assume the worst."

I nod. "Absolutely not."

"Okay," Kelly says.

I pull the card that came with the shoes from my pocket and examine it. I probably shouldn't handle it too much, because the police might use it as evidence. From what Jack wrote, it sounds like he intentionally went missing. But how he could have arranged that is beyond me.

53

———

I slip the small card that came with the shoes in a clean plastic baggie and label it with a black felt tip marker, showing the date and my address. What began as a search and rescue operation has become a mystery about Jack's activities and underhanded dealings. I'm operating in the dark. There is so much we don't know, and I doubt we'll get to the bottom of this.

I bite my lip. If Jack was here, I doubt he would tell us the truth. When we were married, he had a habit of shuffling his feet and looking down when I quizzed him about where the money came from for his latest pair of prize sneakers. He wanted to attend a sneaker convention two days after Kelly was born, but I shot that idea down.

Buzz says, "I'll store the shoes in the pantry. No one will look there if they break in."

Kelly frowns. "We shouldn't open the front door to anyone."

The dog nuzzles my hand. I say, "The dog will keep us safe."

A gust of wind buffets the house. Windows rattle in frames. A draft creeps past, and a shiver runs up my spine.

I say, "I feel like we have a bunch of pieces that don't go together."

Kelly says, "Yeah, me too."

Buzz holds up a hand. "I'll call the bookstore and say I'm taking tonight off. Let's sit down and map this out, and see if we can figure out where it leads."

Kelly purses her lips. "I'm not convinced Dad was running a scam ripping people off. He told me to be nice to the elderly. He said some of them didn't have enough money to get by, with food costs so high. He always dropped a bag of groceries in the donation box at the grocery store."

I resist the urge to roll my eyes. Her father was no saint, but she's making him out to be that way. But she needs to believe in his good nature, so I clamp my mouth shut.

"Okay," I say, "We'll make a list of things like the violin and sneakers that were just delivered, and we'll figure this out. I wonder if we should call Violet and let her know about the note and the shoes."

Buzz says, "I'll let work know I won't be coming in. They can cover for me."

Kelly says, "And I'll let my teacher know I won't be there for dance class this evening."

I wince. I forgot about her class. I've got to up my game to be a good mother and solve the mystery of her missing dad. My phone rings, and I answer it. "This is Irena Fishbone. How can I help you?"

"Our sail ripped, the engine quit, and we're drifting to shore. Can you give us a tow to the marina?" A man sounds rattled and is short of breath.

I glance at Kelly and Buzz. I was looking forward to sorting through what we know and working together. I say into the phone, "Yes, we can help you. What's your position? And I need a credit card for a deposit."

I get his information, grab my purse, and go to the door, waving to Kelly and Buzz. "Sorry, guys, but I have to take this call. I'll be back as soon as I can."

Kelly frowns and folds her arms. "You need an employee, so you have back up."

Buzz nods and shoves his hands in his pockets.

"I can't afford to hire one yet."

They look disappointed, but I've got to go. The dog rubs against my leg, as if begging me to stay. I zip up my rain jacket and say, "I wish I didn't have to help this guy, but I do. If I don't get out there fast, the vessel will sink and so will my business. Love you guys, I've got to run."

I grip the door knob and am about to turn it when Kelly says, "But what about the note? The one in Dad's bedroom? We were going to read it."

"Hold off on that until I come back. I'll see you later." I throw them an air-kiss.

I open the door and step out on the front step. Wind rushes past my cheeks. I glance inside with regrets, because I'd rather be snug and warm with them than going to the rescue. Maybe I'm addicted to drama and being a fixer of disaster. With my knee in the doorway, so the dog won't escape, I say, "Love you, got to go."

"Remember to call Violet," Buzz says. "Tell her about the shoes and the card."

"I will."

They stand like statues and lift their arms in a slow-motion wave. Why is it when I'm in a hurry, time stands still and others don't catch the urgency of helping a boater in distress? Every second counts. My business is life or death.

I frown. The last few moments passed in a flash but felt like an hour. My guilt about leaving loved ones when we were about to tackle a what-the-heck-is-going-on project mixed with major regrets leaves an unsettling stew churning in my gut.

I close the door, make sure it's shut, and run to my car. Rain drops splat down on my scalp and pepper my face. I yank up the hood of my jacket and hurry ahead. Rain drips into my eyes as I unlock the car.

I slide into the driver's seat, slam the car door, and drive off. Given the weather, I should've expected a call. Gale force winds are blowing, and when that happens, trouble kicks up on the water. I wonder why the boater was caught in bad weather. Any sane person would've taken shelter in a hidden cove or never left the marina. This is a good day to sit and nurse a cup of coffee, read a book, or watch TV.

I turn into the marina parking lot and chew the inside of my cheek as a thought skitters past. I hope Jack isn't alive and suffering in the storm. It would be tough to wait for rescue in a marsh, on a beach, or in a driftwood shelter. I hop out, lock the car, and run for my boat.

54

Wind howls from the north, and I drive my boat through white caps to where the skipper is in trouble. Low hanging dark clouds scud overhead. A wave crashes over the bow, and water splashes up on the windshield. The wipers groan.

A sailboat bobs up and down ahead. I nod and lay out a plan in my head. I'll secure a tow line and bring the boat into the marina in the storm. I check my life vest snaps, making sure they are fastened. The life vest inflates automatically if I hit the water, and I changed out the CO_2 cartridge after being swept off Craig's boat. I'm ready.

I go out on deck and put down fenders to protect the boats. Wind whistles past my ears. Salt water sprays my face. Adrenaline surges through me, and I grin. I can do this.

I bring my boat alongside the vessel in distress and

call to the skipper, who is standing in the stern, "Permission to board?"

"Yes," he says. His glasses are fogged up. His yellow rain jacket flaps in the wind.

I lash my boat to his at midships and climb aboard. "Sir, I'll tow you side by side until we're closer to the marina in a quieter cove. I'll change the lines and finish towing you into the marina."

He wipes his forehead. "Sounds good."

Before long, we're heading into the marina. Wind roars, boat masts moan, halyards clang in an eerie setting. This is not a time to be outside, but a time to be in my house with loved ones. I can't wait to get home. I tuck his boat into a slip, and he wraps his lines around dock cleats.

"I'll be back," I call to him. I dock my boat and stride over, lugging my tool kit to the sailboat.

He says, "I have no idea why the engine quit. Hope you can figure it out."

I take a look, unkink a pinched fuel line, and tighten the fuel line couplings and connectors. "Your fuel line was kinked, and the engine was starved for fuel. I suggest you hire a boat mechanic to replace the fuel hose. Use a fuel additive that eliminates bacteria in the tank, if you're not ready already doing that."

He nods, and we shake hands. He says, "Thanks for coming out in this weather."

"You bet. It's what I do. Happy to help."

I carry my tool kit to my boat, stow it, and hurry to my

car. When I'm a few blocks from home, Kelly calls and says, "When are you going to get here?"

She sounds impatient, and I don't blame her. I want to wrap my mind around what is going on. We need an uninterrupted block of time to lay it all out and make sense of what we know. And I need to call Violet, but I'll do that when I'm home.

I say, "I'm on my way. Be there soon." But my mouth falls open as I drive by Craig. His car is parked on the side of the road, and he is standing in the rain talking to the fake pizza delivery guy, who is in a red car. I hunch down in the seat, so they won't see me.

Kelly is still on the line, so I say, "Stay inside, and don't go out. The guy with a gun is driving around town. See you soon."

I hang up and let out a sob. Our situation is hopeless, if our friend is working with the thug who threatened us. Will we ever be safe after this? Can I let my daughter walk to school? I shake my head. Not while everything is up in the air.

I grip the wheel tight, and my childhood haunts my thoughts. If only an adult had protected me, especially on the playground. "Pickle," they yelled, chasing me at recess. "You're a smelly pickle."

I grit my teeth and vow to protect my daughter with my last breath. With a loud thud, a branch falls of the roof of the car and rolls off as I keep going. My hands tremble.

What if Craig is behind all this and orchestrated my nightmare?

I pull up and park at the house. The game is more dangerous with a gun in the picture and knowing Craig is working against us. I hop out and hurry to the door. It flies open, and Kelly runs into my arms. Buzz looks on and says, "Welcome home."

I say, "We've got a lot to talk about."

Buzz hugs us, and I inhale his smell of old books and espresso. I wish I could stay in his arms forever. But like fixing an engine, I'm driven to figure out what is going on. I say, "I could use some hot chocolate."

Buzz steps away and says, "Sit and rest. I'll get you some cocoa." He goes in the kitchen, and I shrug off my rain jacket and sink into the sofa, releasing a sigh. "It's good to be home and out of the wind and rain."

I pat the couch cushion, and Kelly plops down next to me. She says, "Did you call Violet and tell her about the shoes and card we got today?"

I say, "I didn't have time. It was nasty out there. I'll call her in a few minutes."

"That's okay," she says. "Let's see what we know first, and then call her."

I pat her knee and smile. "You sound like you're the one in charge."

Buzz hands us steaming mugs of cocoa, and I cradle mine in my hands to warm my cold fingers. He sets his mug on the coffee table and gives his dog a tussle, saying sweet words. I smile. Watching him play with his dog makes me want him in my life. He is a good man. He's kind to his animal, and he treats me well. We're just going through a rough patch.

Buzz straightens up and says, "Okay, what do we know?"

He opens a closet door, pulls out a whiteboard and markers, and sets it up on my desk in the living room, leaning against a wall.

I tilt my head and give him a half-smile. "You just happened to have that hidden in my closet? Are you in the business of giving lectures and didn't tell me?"

He winks at me and flashes a smile. "You never know when you might need to organize your thoughts about a marketing plan for the bookstore. Or a plan to win a girl-friend you've known for a long time."

My face heats, and I throw him a kiss. "Enough sweet talk. Let's get started. Let's go over everything we know."

He holds up a black marker. I take a deep breath. Finally, we are about to get down to business and hope-fully crack the confusing clues we found. So many unknowns are swirling around.

I sip hot chocolate and lick my lips. Buzz smiles at me, like when we are kids. I grin at him, feeling safe and warm in my home, surrounded by love. Beside me, Kelly pulls out a pen and notebook, poised to take notes.

"Okay," I say. "We'll hammer away at this, and then call Violet if we come up with anything. She does need to know about the shoe delivery and the note. And the fact that I suspect Craig is working with the fake pizza guy with a gun."

Buzz's eyes open wide. Kelly gasps. The dog opens an eye and stares at me.

They both blurt out, "Tell us now."

I say, "I will, but right now, let's start at the beginning. What do we know? Let's list all the clues we can think of."

55

Rain pelts the front windows. Beams in the attic creak and moan as wind batters the house. But that doesn't distract us. We are focused and curious as we assemble clues about what Jack was up to before he disappeared. I'd like to understand what Craig's motivation is in all this, but maybe it comes from pure greed.

On the white board, we list clues. Secret numbers in a plastic potato (Buzz was shocked to hear about that); a note under the end table in Jack's bedroom (Kelly and I agree we must look at that right away after we write the clues down); mysterious deposits into Jack's checking account, and payments made of matching amounts; Craig being in Jack's place several times, searching for something; Craig seen talking with the pizza gunman; the fake pizza guy wanted to hurt us and get something from Jack's apartment; the slashed cushions and break in at Jack's; Craig spotted leaving Jack's apartment carrying a box.

Kelly points to the white board. "We forgot about the naked man in the marsh."

Buzz's right eye twitches. I study him and decide he doesn't know more than he's letting on. We're all tired from the ordeal of not knowing where Jack is and why people want whatever is at Jack's place.

Kelly says, "Write down the blinking light Mom saw under the bridge." She turns to me. "You thought it was suspicious, didn't you?"

I cock my head. "At the time, but now I'm not sure. I could've imagined it."

"But I saw it too," she says. "I have a feeling Dad isn't dead. We've got to figure this out and find him."

To temper her expectations, so she doesn't come crashing down later, I say, "Okay, I'll write that down. But let's remember not every mystery gets solved. The police have tons of cold cases."

Buzz rolls his eyes. "And you call me a downer. It's hard on Kelly."

She says, "Yeah, Mom, thanks for making me feel worse about the situation."

I stand and take the marker from Buzz. "I just want us to be realistic. We'll try our best, but we might not find your dad."

They groan. The dog whines and whimpers, having a dream.

I write on the board, adding the shirt with the writing on the collar that was nailed to the floating log. I scribble about the card that arrived today with the shoes. I write, "He doesn't want to be found?"

Kelly blinks, and for a moment, I think she's going to break down in tears. But she stands tall with her shoulders back, like I taught her. We must be strong to get through life, strong and resilient and able to stand on our own while also relying on others. I bite my lip and realize I could be better at relying on and trusting others.

Kelly says, "If he left on purpose, he'll send for me. I know it."

I scribble on the board, "Motivations for disappearing: Money. Debt. Sneaker addiction."

"Mom, what're you doing?"

I make a face. "Your dad ran up quite a credit card bill buying the shoes in his second bedroom." I frown because it frosts me to know he squandered money that he could have spent on child support. And how selfish to take over the second bedroom for his shoe collection. Kelly deserved a private space when she stayed at his place. His shoes had their own room, but his daughter had to sleep on the couch. Talk about having your priorities out of whack.

I tell her, "He owed a lot of money to people, other than the credit card company. He wasn't the best with money."

Her lower lip trembles, and she nods. "I know. I looked

at his papers when he was out of the room a few weeks ago. I couldn't believe how much he owed. I'm never going to be like that when I grow up."

I say, "I know you won't. You're careful with money. And you've seen how over-spending sent your dad's life sideways."

Buzz clears his throat. "Exactly how much does he owe?"

I take a slow breath, wishing Kelly didn't have to hear this. "I believe he owes over two-hundred -thousand dollars on his credit cards."

Buzz's eyes bulge.

I say, "He told me on Craig's boat he owes a lot of money. He bet on a stock, and instead of it going up, it went way down. He told me he owes a hundred-thousand-dollars for a margin call, whatever that is."

Buzz shoves his hands in his pockets. "Maybe the guy with a gun was sent to collect the money, and he trashed Jack's place, looking for cash."

I say, "Could be."

Kelly says, "Maybe the pizza guy didn't find anything, and he came back to hurt us? To leave a message to people who owe money?"

I nod. "That makes sense."

Buzz sinks onto the sofa and leans back, blowing out a breath. "How did he end up owing that much money? And what was he doing with it? I don't get it."

Kelly shakes her head. "Dad didn't make good choices,

did he? Do you think he escaped to get away from people he owed money to?"

I say, "It's a possibility. I've been thinking that too." An idea occurs to me, and I say, "Before we go any further, let's look at the stuff we took from your father's place. Maybe we'll have more of an idea of what's going on."

We snap on disposable gloves that I keep under the kitchen sink for deep cleaning projects and gather around the kitchen table. I want to preserve any incriminating finger prints. I set my phone in front of me, open a zip-lock bag, and pull out a piece of paper from the underside of Jack's bedside table drawer. Just as I'm about to read it, my cell rings. "Violet's calling," I say. "I'd better get it."

I take off the gloves and answer it. "Hi, Violet. Have you learned anything yet?"

"Yep," she says. "Anything new there?"

I nod. "A pair of shoes and a note were delivered to my house today from Jack."

She says, "I'd like to examine those and bring you up to date. Bring them in and anything else we should know about. We'll go over what we've found." She pauses and says, "This is turning into a bigger project than I thought when I offered to look into it."

I squirm in my seat and hope she won't say she has to charge me for her team's time. I think of my bills. I've been saving to pay the car and boat insurance. Quarterly taxes are due to the IRS. Financially, my nose is above the water line, but I'm not so different than Jack. I'm just better at keeping a job because I am my own boss. But if a glitch happens in the universe and no one goes boating, the incoming tide will pull me under. All it would take is one big unexpected bill, a last wrench in the works.

A shudder runs through me. I don't want to take advantage of another business owner. That wouldn't be right. She runs a company and pays her staff. She can't afford to go in the hole, so I should pay her. I want to figure out what Jack did, clear his name if he wasn't embroiled in a scam, find out where he is and if he disappeared on purpose, and bring him back. That will give us peace of mind. Violet and her team are experts with resources at their fingertips, unlike the three of us at the table. The dog licks my hand, and I don't think he will solve the problems troubling us,

Violet says, "Do you think he left because he owed so much money?"

"Oh, so you found that part out."

"We did. We like doing this sort of thing. It didn't take that much time so far."

I say, "Jack loves Kelly. I don't think he'd run away because he'd miss her too much. But I don't want to take advantage of you, so let me know when I need to start paying you. What's your hourly rate? I hope I can afford it."

Violet says, "I told you I'd look into it as a friend, and I'll keep my word. But I'm thinking about buying a boat.

When I do, how would you feel about giving me free tow and rescue services?"

I laugh. "I didn't expect you to say that, and it's a deal. I appreciate it. I can't wait to hear what you found."

Kelly says, "Let's leave now."

Buzz nods. They stand and start gathering our things to go.

Violet says, "Keep this deal between us because our corporate clients pay high hourly rates and retainers."

I smile. "I won't mention it and thanks. We'll see you soon."

I hang up and look at Kelly and Buzz. They are reading the note. I lean over to see it, but Kelly moves it away from me. I say, "What does it say?"

Buzz frowns. "Not now. We've got to go."

I grab my purse. "Tell me in the car."

Kelly barely hides a smirk as she tucks the note back into the plastic baggie.

Buzz takes a photo of the whiteboard with his phone and sends it to Violet. We load my car with the items that might help solve the puzzle and pile in.

On the five-minute drive, I say, "I can't wait to resolve the questions pecking at my brain like crows at crumbs. I want answers."

Kelly says, "Me too."

Buzz is silent in the back seat. I glance in the rearview mirror, but he won't meet my eyes. His jaw is clenched.

I say, "So what was in the note hidden under your dad's bedside table?"

"You'll find out when we get to Outrigger Services," she says.

Buzz clears his throat. "Craig's looking into Jack's finances bothers me. It's a violation of privacy and flat out wrong."

I say, "I agree. I'm so over it with him."

He gives me a strained smile, but deep down, his comment strikes me as an evasive maneuver designed to distract me from the note taped to the bedside table.

My phone rings, and it is my best friend Abby, who is away at a work event. Buzz says, "Don't answer it. We don't have time to talk."

I answer it anyway and drive by Violet's building, looking for a place to park. "Hey," I say. "I've missed you."

Buzz rolls his eyes.

Abby says, "Miss you too, but I'm having fun at the ice cream convention. I wish Kelly had come with me."

I say, "It's a good thing she didn't because her dad is missing. Did you hear that?"

"Oh, no. What happened?"

"I can't go into it now. We'll talk when you come back." I hang up and park.

Buzz glowers and opens his door. I shake my head and get out of the car. I'm getting fed up with his sour attitude and not sure we'll last another day. I hope our relationship isn't a broken engine beyond repair.

56

———

We hustle up the stairs to Outrigger Services' offices. Kelly glances at me with a look of concern. "Everything okay?"

I nod. "I'm just worried about your dad. I have so many unanswered questions."

"Yeah. me too," she says.

Violet holds the door open as we file in carrying items. She says, "We're meeting in the bullpen. Set those things on the table in the middle of the room." She turns to Buzz. "The photo of the whiteboard was very helpful. We'll go through that together."

She claps her hands. "Okay, team, let's gather round and get started. We'll start by telling you what we know, and then we want to hear from you. From what I saw from what Buzz sent, you have a lot to tell us."

We plunk down in chairs, and Mimi offers us beverages, but we decline. I'm too nervous to drink anything. My chest is tight, and my pulse pounds in my ears.

Violet says, "Go ahead and tell them what we found, Vincent."

He stands. He biceps bulge when he picks up a piece of paper. I'd like to be a report in his hands any day. His gold wedding band flashes in the light, bringing me back to the present.

"Jack was deep in debt," he says. "He owed money to tough characters, who are not the forgiving type. They don't let debts go unpaid. They'll kill to make a statement. It looked to us like Jack had no way to repay his debt to them or the investment firm or the credit card companies. He was maxed out on five credit cards."

I hold Kelly's hand and wish she didn't have to hear this, but it's important she know the truth. She'd only hound me at home if I didn't bring her with me.

Buzz says, "Five credit cards, but he never paid for dinner."

I nod. The man knew how to mooch. For Jack, it was a shameless art form.

"We're used to uncovering debt, so that didn't surprise us. What gave us a jolt was how he left a trail of bread-crumbs, if you will, in digital form, to tell us what he planned and where he might be."

Kelly, Buzz, and I gasp. I say, "You think he might be alive?"

Violet nods, and her dark eyes flicker with concern.

"We're not sure, but that's where the data is leading us. Go on, Vincent."

He shrugs. "I'm sorry to tell you this, but it looks like he escaped to start a new life." He turns to Mimi. "Want to take over the debrief?"

She says, "Sure. What we found." But she is interrupted by a knock at the door, and we all look that way.

Craig barges into the room. "I have a right to hear what you're saying if you're talking about me." He holds up his hands. 'No matter what Irena and Buzz say, I'm innocent. I didn't do anything. I was hanging at Jack's place, remembering old times."

A tear trickles down his cheek, and I swear he must have found a way to manufacture the waterworks. What a jerk. He must have followed us here. He hasn't seemed sad for a second since Jack fell overboard. I hope he burns in whatever hell is reserved for liars and people who are cold-hearted enough to deceive their closest friends.

I stand and point to the door. "Get out of here. This is our meeting. We didn't invite you."

He stares at me and scratches a two-day stubble on his chin. It sounds like sandpaper scraping something, like he's getting on my nerves now. I step close, hold his gaze, and say, "I seriously doubt you're sorry about Jack being missing, so cut out the crying act. You've been digging through Jack's papers. We heard you carried a box from his apartment to your car. You're hunting for something. What're you up to?"

Instead of answering, he turns to the photo of the white board Violet hung up and jabs a finger at a line item. He rounds on Buzz. "What did the card say that delivered to her house today?"

Buzz crosses his arms, and his muscles flex. His jaw tenses. "Have you been watching her house? How did you know things were delivered?"

Violet steps in between them and ushers Craig out of the room. He turns and glares at our group before slamming the door shut behind him. She locks the door and comes back to join us. In my mind, if someone proclaims their innocence, they are guilty as all get out. I frown. Craig has always been out for himself and eager to make a buck. It sounded like he was watching my house, which sends shivers down my spine.

Violet says, "We could've asked Craig to join us, but at this point, I'd like to keep the group small to control the flow of information and stop gossip spreading, with fewer voices weighing in. We'll contact Craig later if we need to."

I roll my eyes. "Good luck stopping small-town gossip. It's an unending river you'll never damn up."

Buzz chuckles and reaches over, taking my hand in his. We'll find Jack, dead or alive, with Violet and her team's help, and end the madness of mysterious messages arriving by courier.

Violet says, "Mimi, what were you about to say before we were interrupted?"

57

———————

Mimi clears her throat. "Let's get through this and take questions afterwards." She turns to me and says, "Your ex-husband was hiding a lot of secrets. Are you sure you want your daughter to listen to this? She might learn things about her father that you wish she didn't know."

I blow out a breath and wonder if I'm being the best mother by having Kelly exposed to truths about her dad that she'd be better off not knowing. I say to Kelly, "Maybe you shouldn't be here. I shouldn't have brought you along. We don't know what they found."

She stares at me, her eyes pleading. She clutches my arm and holds on with a vise-like grip. "I have to stay. I want to know. I need to ask questions about what Dad was doing. Don't treat me like a child."

When I hesitate, she says, "Please, let me stay."

Buzz whispers to me, "Maybe she should sit in the car while we talk."

I make up my mind and hope I won't regret my decision later. To Kelly, I say, "Fine, you can stay. I'd tell you most or all of it later anyway, so you might as well hear it first-hand."

Mimi nods and taps on her laptop keyboard. An image of Jack comes up at an ATM machine. I open my mouth to ask questions, but she holds up an index finger and says, "We'll take questions later. Here's what we found. Jack used an ATM in town the morning he was swept overboard. He withdrew four hundred dollars, which was almost all he had in his checking account. You see how he's pulling his cap over his eyes? He's trying not to be caught by the video surveillance, but he failed."

She taps her laptop, and the image changes. "As I believe you know, he was fired from his last job three months ago."

He didn't mention he was fired," I say.

Mimi continues. "That must've made him desperate for money to pay rent and buy food. But then Craig stepped in to pay his rent. And from Jack's credit card bills, we know he has a flair for buying very expensive shoes. He owes over two hundred fifty thousand dollars on his credit cards."

I wipe my sweaty palms on my jeans. This is worse than I thought.

"From what we gather," Violet interjects, "he turned to

the mob for a cash infusion. But the trouble is, interest was adding up on that debt and the credit cards faster than he could pay it back."

I shake my head. Stupid, stupid Jack.

Mimi says, "Jack was in over his head, and we believe he owed more than a half million dollars when he went overboard. We suspect he planned his disappearance and doesn't want to be found. He's hiding from creditors and the mob, and we don't think he's coming back."

I let out a heavy sigh, and Kelly does the same. I glance at Buzz and a satisfied smile crosses his face, but he wipes it away with his hand.

Vincent says, "There's one other odd thing about this case. Deposits into his bank account and out each month confused us. It almost looked like he was running a scam on older retired people and turning the money over to someone."

I clench my jaw. Jack wouldn't take advantage of senior citizens. He could turn on the charm whenever he wanted, and generally get whatever he wanted, whether it was for someone to pay for his dinner, have a free drink on the house, or get a ride to his apartment. I used to tease him and call him Jack Prince Charming when we were married. I blink away tears.

Buzz leans over and says, "Don't cry. This is good news. He's alive. It's what you wanted, isn't it?"

Kelly grips my hand. "Dad wouldn't do that, would he?"

I say in a low voice to her, "I don't know. I hope not. Let's listen."

Buzz flashes me a concerned look and laces his fingers in front of him.

Vincent says, "But something didn't make sense to us. The scams he was running weren't enough to pay off his tremendous debt to the banks and the mob. So, why would he do it and take the risk of getting caught and being thrown in prison? Especially in light of his love for his daughter."

Kelly tightens her grip, and I pull away, shaking out my hand.

Mimi chimes in. "We suspect he was working undercover for a federal agency."

Violet says, "We don't have proof and may never have it, that he entered the witness protection program in exchange for providing information. He may have arranged his disappearance and had help with it."

She looks at Buzz and holds his gaze. "I believe you helped Jack get out of town. Surveillance cameras at the marina show you getting in your boat after Jack disappeared and bringing him back to the dock. Then you drove off with him in your car."

I flinch. A chill sweeps up my spine. My hands clench, and I turn to Buzz. "Is this true? Did you help Jack disappear?"

His Adam's apple bobs up and down. He coughs, covering his mouth with his fist.

"Don't avoid the question," I say. "Did you help Jack leave? You did, didn't you? What were you thinking?"

He shakes his head. "It was the right thing for all of us. You'll see it someday. I did it so the three of us could be happy together, you, me, and Kelly. With him out of the picture, we're finally a family."

I slap his face. "Damn you for thinking you can make life decisions for us. We love that man."

Kelly weeps beside me. I shake Buzz by the shoulders for depriving us of Jack's presence. "Where did you take him?"

Rubbing his face where I slapped him, he says, "He's somewhere he won't be found."

He tries to hold my hand, but I shove it away.

Through clenched teeth, I say, "Where is he?"

"Listen, the mob was after him and was going to kill him. He made bad choices, and this is what he got. Believe me, this is best. You'll see that in time."

"You'll regret this. As of this moment, we're done. I'm sorry I ever got together with you." I turn to Kelly and say, "I'm sorry all this happened."

A vein pulses on Buzz's forehead. He says, "You were distracted by him. All the times you ran to meet him between rescue jobs. It was never just you and me. I was in the middle of your relationship with him. I was the interloper. You wouldn't stop talking about him. Now it will be just be the two of us in a relationship."

I snort. "He is the father of my child and my ex-husband. I think I have reason to talk about him and see him whenever I want."

Kelly says, "Yeah, that's right, you do."

I scowl at Buzz, "If you loved me, you wouldn't have helped him escape."

He says, "The reason I helped him escape is I know how you feel about him and you'd want him alive."

I grip his knee, digging in my fingernails. "Where did you take him? I've got to find him."

He stands and says, "I don't know where he is. You're better off without him, both of you. He didn't tell me where he was going after I dropped him off."

Kelly howls and leaps up, pounding on his chest. "You did this. It's your fault. Bring him back now."

Violet steps in and separates them. "Sit down, and let's discuss this. We can't get emotional. We have a lot to figure out before we leave this room. We need clear heads."

I take Kelly's arm and guide her to a chair. "She's right. Let's keep going and find out what they know."

We sit side by side clutching each other's hands. Her body trembles. I must be strong for her, learn where Jack is and convince him to come back.

Buzz takes a seat on the other side of the room and rubs his cheek with a surly expression on his face. I shake my head at him. Sorry, Buzz, but we're through. I'll pack your things in my house, dump them outside, and never see you again.

He proposed last week, and I laughed and said we didn't need to rush things. We could take it slow. He said he'd hoped I'd say yes right away and jump on the idea of planning a wedding.

Violent crosses her arms. "Buzz, do you know where Jack was going? It would be helpful if you told us, so we don't have to take the trouble to look into it."

He says, "He wouldn't tell me, and I didn't want to know. He's better off gone. I just wanted my girlfriend to myself. Is that too much to ask?"

I say, "You selfish, selfish man. What were you thinking, ruining our lives so you'd be happier?"

He opens his hands. "I wasn't trying to ruin your lives. I was just helping him escape. If that made our relationship better, I was all for it."

Violet says, "Let's leave the part about where Jack is for now. We might be able to find him through other means. Mimi, do you want to finish up the client summary?"

Mimi brightens. "You bet, boss. Okay, we've established that Jack had debts he couldn't repay. We believe he was working for the authorities to uncover a scam. And he wanted to disappear. The writing on his shirt collar points to that."

"The note we got today said that too," I say. Turning to Kelly, I add, "At least we know he's alive, and that's great news."

Buzz says, "It's not like he is a piece of lost luggage you

can track down. You shouldn't bother. He'll be safer this way."

Victor says, "Let's look at what you brought. It might fill in missing gaps and give us answers."

My stomach knots. Shame on Jack for getting himself in this mess. He spent beyond his means, went deep in debt to the wrong people and abandoned his daughter.

58

We set items on a table in the bullpen at Violet's. There is the note from Jack's bedside table, and the shoebox that arrived today with the mysterious, confounding note. I haul out a plastic garbage bag I brought along with the Reader's Digest book I took from Jack's place. At the last minute, I go all-in and place the plastic baggie with the numbers on a slip of paper on the table and what I believe is a password. Vincent leans over and studies it. "What's that? And where'd you find it?"

I glance at the odd assortment of stuff on the table. I glare at Buzz, sending him a sizzling, searing stare. Don't bother knocking, because this boat has left the dock.

Buzz holds up his hands and looks at me. I make a sour face, shaking my head. No excuses, buster. Not this time, not ever. Our common bond over both being teased for our names in grade school has been shredded. Bud Wiser, my former boyfriend and dear friend, deceived me and helped Jack leave town. I ran around searching for a body, but he knew what had happened all along.

I say, "The scrap of paper with numbers was hidden in Jack's refrigerator, in a plastic potato, if you can believe it." I laugh, partly to release tension, and the others join in. "I bet it wasn't there a few weeks ago, was it, Kelly?"

Her gaze flickers to Buzz, and she frowns before answering. Damn him for thinking this would solidify our relationship. We almost became a newly formed family of three, but we have crashed and burned to the ground.

Kelly says, "I never saw it before. He must've put it there before we went out on the boat."

I say, "Are those numbers for an offshore bank account, do you think?"

Violet says, "Given what's been going on, it's highly likely. We'll look into it. And this might be the password."

I say, "It was in the freezer with a frozen pizza."

I shoot Kelly a look and offer my hand. She grasps mine, holding it tight, standing by my side. Buzz is three feet away on the other side of the table.

Violet points to the blue and green Reader's Digest book. "Okay if I open this?"

Kelly says, "No, wait. Not yet. Let's open the note from my dad's bedside table."

I nod. I've been wondering what it said.

Violet says to my daughter, "Why don't you do the

honors?" She hands her a pair of disposable gloves, and Kelly grins, pulling them on. She plucks the note from the plastic bag and opens it.

I lean over to read. I see my name, but I can't make out the rest because tears blur my vision. The enormity of what's happened, Jack fleeing his debt, and the loss of my budding romance with Buzz sweeps over me. I stifle a sob. This is not the time and place to implode. I'll save it for later, when I'm out on my boat alone, with only the wind and waves to witness my unraveling. "What does it say?"

Buzz comes over and hugs me, but I step away. I cross my arms and take a slow breath to steady myself. Everything I loved about my life with my group of long-time friends is gone. My life is bursting into flames and burning down to the waterline.

Kelly says in a choked voice, "The note says he loved you, and you were the love of his life. That he hated to leave us. He's sorry his obsession with sneakers drove you away."

My throat closes tight. I say, "I loved him. We just couldn't live together. I wish he had sold the shoes and stayed in town. It would've worked out better for all of us."

Buzz says, "This will be better. You'll see."

I shake my head. "Sorry, Buzz, but we're through. By helping Jack leave and not telling me, you ended what we had."

Kelly sets down the note, takes off her gloves and turns away, bursting into tears.

Violet claps her hands. "Come on, people. We've got to stay on task, or we'll never get through this. Irena, do you think the money from selling Jack's sneaker collection will pay off his debts?"

I purse my lips and consider the amount they might bring in before nodding. Over the years I've researched Jack's habit, his addiction to shoes, and kept tabs on how much he could have sold them for, so I'm ready for this question.

"Definitely, yes. I think I could sell them, pay it off, and keep the pizza thug away from our door. Especially with the latest shoe that arrived today. It's a Double Guard Half Spin Super Splat Signed sneaker from a limited edition."

I snap on a disposable glove and open the shoe box that arrived today. A murmur runs around the room. The gold leather shoe fairly glows.

Vincent whistles. "Never thought I'd see a pair of those in my lifetime. Are you sure they're real?"

I lift the tongue, where a "Limited Edition" stamp is printed with the number one. "Sure am, Maybe Jack can come back after his debts are paid off. It's a long shot though, Kelly, so don't get your hopes up."

I hold up the note that was delivered with the sneakers. "This arrived with the latest shoes, and it says basically what the writing on the shirt collar said. He doesn't want to be found."

Mimi holds out a gloved hand. "I'll take that. We'll have it analyzed for fingerprints and see if the hand writing is a match for Jack's. You never know, someone might be holding Jack hostage and faking the notes and the writing on the shirt collar, until they're ready to send a ransom note."

I let out a choked cackle. Kelly stares at me and says, "This isn't funny."

I hold up my hands. "Sorry, it struck me as odd that anyone would kidnap Jack. We're not wealthy. And it's been a long time since he disappeared. Wouldn't a ransom note be delivered by now?"

Vincent says, "Not always." He turns to Buzz. "You saw him last. When was that? Was anyone with him? Where did you drop him off?"

Buzz slumps into a seat. "He made me promise not to tell you. He didn't want people looking for him, like the guy with the gun."

59

———

Vincent slams a fist on the table. "Tell us. You were the last person to see Jack alive. Tell us exactly what went down that day."

We sit, and my knees tremble. Kelly and I hold hands. Buzz mumbles.

Violet raps on the table. "Speak up. We can't hear you. Talk to us."

He says, "I picked him up in my boat, when I was supposed to be searching in a different area. He was standing under Jackson Bridge on a little beach, and I took him a few miles west of town to a run-down cannery building on the water. No one was around. He changed into a wool sweater, a coat and jeans and boots. He told me he hid them in a backpack near the marsh. It was part of his plan to escape."

Violet says, "Where was he going? Did he mention anyone else helping him?"

Buzz squirms in his seat. "I got the impression the authorities were helping him, but later I decided it was far-fetched and dismissed the idea. I mean, why would they be interested in a small-time guy like Jack?"

Mimi says, "We have reason to believe Jack was helping investigate a multi-state scam, defrauding the elderly of funds. You may have heard of the phone calls senior citizens have been getting, where they're offered a chance to buy stocks at a deep discount, and they're guaranteed to double their money within thirty days."

I lick my lips. If Jack was working to prevent scams like this, he wasn't a bad guy after all. Maybe he was righting wrongs while finding a way to leave his debts behind.

Violet says, "We alerted the FBI to our suspicions about this scam a month ago. We believe Jack has been working undercover for them."

My eyes open wide. "Does that mean Craig will be arrested for his part in the scam?"

Mimi looks up from her phone. "Our sources say Craig was arrested minutes ago. I don't think you'll be seeing him for a long time."

I sink back in a chair, and my hands drop to my sides. "So, you're not expecting a ransom note?"

Vincent says, "We don't think so. We believe the authorities are hiding him until this all blows over."

Whooshing out a breath, I say, "I didn't expect to hear that. Thank you for looking into this."

Mimi says, "So that's a wrap, then, I guess."

Violet holds up an index finger. "Not so fast. What's in the Reader's Digest book you took from Jack's place? Might be something we need to know in there."

I say, "Go ahead, take a look."

"Wait, not yet," Kelly says. "I have something to look at first." She pulls a violin case from a black plastic garbage bag. "I took this from Dad's at the last minute." She clicks the case open. Inside, a beautiful violin rests on a purple velvet.

I swallow hard, because I've always wanted to learn to play the violin, and Jack knew it. I haven't mentioned it to Buzz.

Kelly says, "There is a note inside." She hands it to Violet. "You can read it."

Violet reads the note aloud. "For Irena Fishbone, my one and only best wife. May you play for years and let your heart soar with music that makes the angels sing. Ask the violin maker. He knows the secrets behind this story. Your one and only, Jack"

Tears clog my throat. Kelly says, "Now you can play. You've always wanted a violin. Maybe the violin maker can give you lessons."

I nod. "We'll see."

"Moving on," Vincent says as he opens the Reader's Digest book. It is hollowed out, and inside is a fortune cookie wrapped in cellophane. I nudge my daughter with an elbow. "Go ahead, open it. That's your favorite cookie."

Her lips tremble as she opens the cookie and pulls out a fortune.

Vincent says, "What does it say?"

Kelly says in a shaking voice, "Love you, Kelly, with all my heart. I'll be back for you some day."

I say, "Whatever happens, you're the best and most beautiful, super smart person I could ever be a mother to. We'll be fine, just the two of us."

Buzz crosses his arms and glares. Violet nods. Kelly and I gather our things to go. I thank Violet and her team and turn to open the door.

Buzz says, "Wait for me."

I shrug. "You're on your own. I'll pack your stuff up tonight and put it out on the curb, if you want to get it. Otherwise, I'll take it to the dump. Family is thicker than jealous love. Goodbye, former friend."

With that, my daughter and I walk out the door to begin the rest of our lives. I've lost my friends. My former husband left town. And I have the honor of raising my daughter alone until Jack returns to town, if he ever does.

We walk down the street to my car in the pouring rain.

Kelly says, "Do you think we should've offered Buzz a ride?"

I say, "He can walk to his house from here. We've seen enough of him for a long time. I don't need a jealous love in my life."

She smiles. "We'll be fine on our own."

We carefully place the violin in the back of my car. The storm is blowing, making boat halyards clash against masts. It is possible this isn't over yet, but I'll find a way forward and overcome against the odds, no matter what is next.

I drive to my house and turn on the radio. As we sing along, I glance over at my daughter. Although the writing on Jack's shirt collar said he didn't want to be found, I pray that there will be a time when he comes back because Kelly needs him in her life.

BUZZ

I PULL up the hood of my jacket and jog in the rain to my house. Irena drives by, but she doesn't see me. I'm just another stranger on the sidewalk. When her taillights disappear around the corner, I throw off my hood and tip my head back, cackling.

She bought it. They all bought the story, the fibs, the lies, and the fabrication. I helped Jack set up his disappearance and drove the older woman painter to the marsh, towing her dinghy behind my boat. She was there to divert attention from Jack and distract searchers, and she did a fine job of it. Paying her for the acting job was well worth it in order for Jack to escape.

I start jogging to my house, rain dripping down into my eyes. I laid the clues, and I'm cleverer than they suspected. My goal was to get Jack out of town, so I had Craig rope him into the scam early on. I smile to myself, because I know I'll get Irena back. She loves me and has always cared for me. Such a long-time bond can't be put asunder so easily.

But she can never know I left Jack on the pavement, blood oozing from his head after I hit him and he fell back. I'd done him plenty of favors, helped him plan the clues for his sudden disappearance. But when he babbled about taking Irena and Kelly with him and going back to get them at her house before he left town, I couldn't help myself.

I smacked his jaw as hard as I could. His head snapped back. He stumbled and fell on his head. The sound was sickening, but he deserved it. I couldn't stand by and let him take my new family away from me. No one gets away with that. No one. Not even my best friend.

I walk in my house, which smells musty after being closed up, and hang my dripping coat on a hook in the hall. Striding into my second bedroom, my shoes are wet, but I don't care. I pull a metal key from my pocket, unlock the closet door, and let out a sigh. The dream will take longer to achieve than I had planned. Jack kept a shrine to shoes, but I have a secret shrine to my love.

I light a candle and smile at the silver framed photo

taken in grade school. "We'll get back together, Irena. I love you, and I'm the only man for you."

IRENA

I DRIVE past Buzz on the street on the way home and see him laughing in the rain. "That's weird," I say to Kelly. "Did you see Buzz back there? He was laughing."

She says, "When we were at Violet's, I felt like he knew something he wasn't telling us. He wiped a smile off his face a few times."

A sudden cold fear grips me, and a shiver runs down my spine. An inner knowing gnaws deep within. I am suddenly certain that Buzz killed Jack and lied to cover it up.

When the dust settles from the last few frantic days, I will make it my life's work to uncover what happened to Jack and expose Buzz.

Thank you for reading this! If you enjoyed *Under Jackson Bridge*, please let other readers know what to expect by posting reviews on Goodreads, Amazon and Bookbub.

Sign up at www.susanspechtoram.com for my newsletter to be the first to hear about my new books. We'll never share your email and you can unsubscribe at any time.

Interested in Violet's and Karina's stories? Read the *Family Secrets Series* (with *The Mother's Threat and Secrets at the Café*)!

Under Jackson Bridge is the first book in a new thriller series. Pre-order the next book, *Missing Man*, and be the first to read the page-turner!
Stay tuned for more!

Follow me on BookBub for updates about my new books.

ABOUT THE AUTHOR

Susan is writing mysteries, thrillers, and suspense novels. Previously, she served as senior director of corporate communications for biotechnology companies. Susan worked as an activity aide in an upscale nursing home's psychiatric unit. She was a potter and painter with an art studio in Seattle and has also worked as a market researcher, a nurse's aide, a waitress, and a library page. Her essays have been published in Mothering Magazine, Twins Magazine and Utne Reader.

Susan grew up near Detroit, Michigan and received a BFA with Honors from University of Oregon and a MBA in Marketing from Seattle University. She lives in a windy part of the Pacific Northwest with her husband and their rescue dog.

BOOKS BY SUSAN SPECHT ORAM

Shore Lodge

The Thieves

Cabin Eight

The Mother's Threat

Secrets at the Café

Under Jackson Bridge

Humorous fiction:

Boating with Buddy, a report from a canine correspondent

Nonfiction:

Brief business books on investor relations, crisis
communication and public relations